HUNGER

THE SEDUCTORS SERIES

B. L. WILDE

For Jo, who is on this journey with me every step of the way.

Prologue

"You've done amazingly well, Jade," Sonia praised from her seat behind her desk. Once I'd arrived back at headquarters, she'd requested to see me.

"I told you I'd complete this mission."

"I'm sorry that I ever doubted you."

"Oliver will try everything to find me, though. You'll need to make sure the clean-up crew doesn't leave anything to chance." I had to admit I was worried. I could only *imagine* how he must have reacted to waking up and finding me gone. I couldn't dwell on that, though. It would drive me insane.

"You have nothing to worry about, Jade. You know our defenses are untouchable. Of course, you'll be on lockdown for at least three months, just to be safe." *Three months!* Great!

"Can I help with intelligence while I'm here? I need to be doing *something*." I had to keep myself busy. I couldn't let my mind wander to thoughts of *him*.

"I'm sure Miles would be happy to have you," Sonia mused, "but take a few days to regroup first. You must be exhausted." I was—physically *and* emotionally. "I know it can't have been easy for you." I looked up at Sonia with a frown. "I'm not the heartless bitch everyone thinks I am. I know you formed a bond with Mr. Kirkham."

"It was a bond I was able to break, Sonia. Don't worry about it." She could be trying to trick me, so I wasn't going to openly admit that I'd developed feelings for Oliver.

"You're one of the strongest Seductors I have. I need to make sure you won't do anything stupid."

"If I'm on lockdown for three months, I can't see myself getting into any trouble."

"It happens to all Seductors at some point, Jade. All you need to do is focus on your work—it will help you to let go. Hell, it might even make you *more* dedicated, if that's at all possible."

"This won't affect my work," I assured. "It was just sex. Okay, it may have been *great* sex, but that's still all it was."

Sonia eyed me carefully before she spoke again. "I will let you know once the blueprints have been received by our client. This mission will be a good pay out for you. Why don't you take a nice vacation and clear your head before you go on lockdown? We'll just need to make sure the location is untraceable." I nodded, but it didn't feel right knowing I was going to be getting money by betraying Oliver. I'd never had this feeling about a mission before. "That's all for now, thank you."

I walked out toward the pool to find Georgie. She was sitting in one of the lounge chairs reading a book until she spotted me.

"How did it go?" she asked warily, getting up.

"The mission is complete."

"Come here, baby girl." She pulled me into a tight hug. "I'm so proud of you. It couldn't have been easy."

"It was pure torture," I whispered into her ear, holding her tighter, "but do you know what the hardest thing is?"

"What?"

"Knowing that right now he'll be trying to find me. It will destroy him when he keeps hitting dead ends. I can't even think about what's crossing his mind right now. We became so close on the last visit, and he told me things I never thought I'd want to hear. Oh, Georgie, the way he loved me...I can't even explain how good it felt." A few of the Seductors around the pool seemed to be watching my mini breakdown with interest, but I didn't care at the moment. It was all starting to hit me—I was never going to see Oliver again.

"Hush," she cooed, rubbing my back comfortingly. "I know it hurts, Jade. We've all been there, but you've done the right thing. We have no other choice until our contracts end."

"I shouldn't have let him fall in love with me. I could have played a bitch so he wouldn't be hurting right now. I could have done this all so differently, but being with him...I...I...I just kept losing myself. I...did it all wrong."

"Stop that!" Georgie snapped, shaking me. "Don't doubt your skills, Jade. There is a reason you're the number one Seductor here. You are *brilliant* at what you do! It wouldn't have mattered what character you played. He still would have fallen for you."

"Have you ever doubted being a Seductor?" I questioned, pulling back from her.

"Is that what all of this is about?" Georgie looked around, knowing this conversation was becoming a little too dangerous. If anyone overheard us, they might report back to Sonia. "Come on, Jelly Bean. I need to grab something from our room," she muttered, noticing Alicia wasn't too far away from us with her head tilted slightly in our direction. Yeah, I knew she was trying to listen in. Alicia had *always* had it in for me. She hated that I

HUNGER

made more money than her and got the first pick of the top jobs. Not to mention I had to clean up her mess on a mission last year.

Molly was out on a mission for a few days, so Georgie and I had the room to ourselves. I loved Molly, I really did, but she was younger than Georgie and I, so she didn't have the same life experiences.

"What is going on in that head of yours?" Georgie had a look of fear in her eyes as she slumped down onto my bed next to me.

"I'm not going to do anything stupid." First Sonia, now Georgie? Jeez! What did they think I was going to do—throw myself at Oliver and beg him to take me back after everything I'd done? The truth was, if I wasn't so ashamed of myself, and it wasn't so dangerous for him, I might have actually considered it.

"Good, because I couldn't watch you being hunted down if you decided to make a run for it. Where would you even go? Back to him?" Damn, she was good. Was I that easy to read right now?

"I'm not even thinking that," I lied.

"Where has this doubt suddenly come from, then?"

"It's not easy to let go of something you've never had before. I guess it's just hard to wrap my head around the fact that it's over."

"Your paths might cross one day when you leave The Seductors. Stranger things have happened." I knew that was true. It was the main clause in the contract that made me sign over five years ago. I had the choice to be Jade Phillips again when I left, or an identity I had been previously for the Seductors. I could even be someone completely new. It was the deal of a lifetime—being able to start all over again, with no baggage to hold you down. Not that it mattered in this case. Oliver wouldn't

4

be available in five years, and I wasn't delusional enough to think he would be. Some amazing woman who actually *deserved* him would have snatched him up by then and would be having amazing sex for the rest of her life. Plus, there was no guarantee I would even be allowed to contact him. And if I could, how would I explain a name change to him? I was sure the Seductors wouldn't allow it anyway. Oliver was a top priority mission. It was too dangerous to go back to those.

"That's never going to happen. I can't sit here thinking about that for the next five years, either. It would drive me insane. I need to forget him."

"And you can do that, can you?"

"I have to," I stressed, running my hands through my hair before getting up to pace the room. "It's going to drive me crazy being cooped up in here for three months."

"How serious are these feelings you have for him, Jade? I've never seen you this worked up before."

Did I tell Georgie the truth? Damn! If I didn't tell her, who could I tell?

"I think I've fallen in love with him." My voice was just a whisper, but saying the words out loud was like stabbing a hot dagger straight through my heart. I loved him; I *really* loved him.

I couldn't let Oliver weaken me, though. Yes, I loved him, but what did that matter now? It could never work. He wasn't in love with *me*, anyway. He loved the Jade I had created for him.

"You. Love. Him?" Georgie's mouth hung open as she gawked at me.

"It doesn't matter now. I'm never going to see him again. Besides, when he discovers what I stole from him, he'll hate me forever. It's better this way."

"Jade, you've fallen in love with someone. You can't just sweep this under the rug. With your past, you know how significant this is."

"Can we not go into my past right now?" I stressed. "This has nothing to do with that."

"Bullshit! It has *everything* to do with that."

"Don't fucking start, Georgie," I threatened. I wasn't prepared to talk about my past right now.

"Jade, it's not a crime to want to be loved. That's what makes the world go 'round."

"It's a little different when the guy you love doesn't actually know the real you."

"There are parts of ourselves in the characters we play. Don't you pay attention to any of the workshops or lessons we have?" She shook her head at me. "Anyway, how do you know the real parts aren't what he loves the most?" She really wasn't helping, and wanting to avoid eye contact, I looked down at the floor. "You see! You can't be sure, can you?"

"None of this matters."

"If you're thinking of leaving the Seductors, I'd say it *all* matters. Jade, you can't run. They'd kill you before you were even out of St. Petersburg. You know the response team is ruthless."

"It's not going to come to that. I'm not going anywhere. I just need time to adjust, that's all."

"Promise you'll call me if you need anything in the next few weeks. I hate having to leave you, but I fly out to Miami on Monday."

"I'll be fine. What trouble am I going to get into here?"

"Please don't keep your feelings inside, Jade. I'll only be a phone call away. If I'm busy, I will call you back as soon as I can."

"I know." I was lucky to have Georgie as my friend. She may be blunt and take no shit from anyone, but she had such a big heart.

"It will get better, Jelly Bean. Trust me." I had to have faith in her words. Besides, right now it couldn't get much worse. The only way to go when you'd hit rock bottom was up.

❉ ❉ ❉

I held my tongue and counted to ten.

"Did you hear me, Jade?" Alicia questioned while my back was to her. How could I *not* have heard her? She was right behind me!

"Your paperwork is almost ready. We just need to run a few more checks and get clearance for your new passport."

"I leave tomorrow morning. This is a big case, so you better tell Miles to hurry up."

"He's going as fast as he can!" I fumed. "Believe it or not, Alicia, your mission isn't the only one we have to prepare for. It will be done. Has Miles ever been late?"

"You're extra bitchy today. Is the lockdown finally getting to you?" Taking a deep breath, I was able to maintain my composure. I wasn't going to stoop to her level and retaliate. Yes, I had been on lockdown for almost four months, but it was for my own safety.

The lengths Oliver had gone to in trying to find me were unbelievable. I don't think a target had *ever* gotten as close to the Seductors as he had, but the organization was too secure to penetrate. Miles was always one step ahead, and even after four months of searching for me, it seemed Oliver wasn't going to admit defeat. Hence me still being on lockdown.

I had no idea if he had learned about the stolen blueprints yet or not. Being trapped at headquarters meant I didn't have much access to the outside world.

"Are you going to speak to Miles, then?" Alicia snapped, flicking her dark hair over her shoulder, snapping me from my thoughts.

"You'll get it in plenty of time. Why don't you go and jump on Mario's dick one last time while you wait? You won't see him for a while, after all," I joked. I had noticed that her paperwork for the new mission spanned six months. It must have been a top assignment for it to be that long. If I hadn't still been on lockdown, I suspected it would have been mine to undertake, but Alicia was running all the large assignments for the time being.

"Fuck you, Jade." Yeah, that was her usual tone toward me.

"I don't have to be nice to you when you're acting like such a bitch, Alicia. I'm just helping Miles out."

"You think you're so special, don't you? Well, I have news for you—I've been assigned the largest mission in Seductor history. It's time you were knocked off the pedestal that Sonia put you on." Alicia had a gleam in her eye as she smirked at me.

"I can guarantee if I wasn't on lockdown, things would be different."

"I'm not so sure about that." Something in her tone made me think she was hiding something—something that involved me. I had always been good at reading people, and Alicia was no different. "Just make sure the paperwork is done." With that, she strutted off, tossing her horse tail hair in my face as she went.

"Argh," I moaned, walking back into the intelligence

office.

"What's up?" Miles called from his computer. He was your typical computer geek, with dark curly hair and big thick glasses. I kept telling him the glasses were too big for his face and that they hid his pretty blue eyes, but he always played it off. I had the feeling I made him a little nervous. He ran the intelligence center here with his team and was a genius.

"Alicia," I snarled. "She is such a bitch."

"What actually went on with you two last year?"

"It's a long story. We'd be here all day."

"Well, you're not going anywhere for a while, are you? You can tell me about it tomorrow. We could even have lunch somewhere low key," Miles suggested. Did he really just ask me out to lunch? I wasn't allowed off these grounds.

"Alicia asked if her paperwork could all be ready first thing in the morning."

"Wow, you really don't want to talk about it, do you?"

"Nope. Is this mission of hers really the biggest in Seductor history?"

"Where did you hear that?" He looked up in alarm from his computer screen.

"Alicia told me."

"She shouldn't be shouting her mouth off like that. It will get her into trouble one day."

"Where is she flying out to tomorrow?" I don't know why I was asking. It wasn't allowed and I knew that, but something was beginning to worry me. I was probably just being paranoid, but Alicia had been deliberately goading me earlier. Why? What did she know that I didn't?

"Why are you asking?"

"I was just curious."

"You know the rules, Jade. You shouldn't pry into other cases. You're becoming as bad as Molly. Why don't you start uploading those files into the database for me? Mandy said she'll be in a little later today to finish them off."

"I don't care about the mission. I'm only curious where she is flying out to."

"New York!" He snapped. "Can I concentrate now? I have thirteen threats on our databases right now, seven fake accounts to create, four prototypes to check, and my mother to call. It's her birthday today. It's not easy running a team of ten people who all think they are science geniuses in these small conditions!" *New York?* I was thinking too much into it. Oliver wasn't the only person who lived in New York. Just because Alicia was going there, that didn't mean *he* was her target.

"Yeah, sorry," I muttered numbly, going back to my desk and ignoring his rant.

It didn't matter how much I tried to shake the thought from my mind, though. Alicia's gloating tone and the fact she was on her way to New York tomorrow kept clouding my mind.

What were the odds? No, it couldn't be. I *was* being paranoid. What would our client want with Oliver again? Surely the blueprints for the machine were enough.

Four months, and I still couldn't get him out of my head. I was even becoming delusional and suspicious. *Oliver, what have you done to me?*

Alicia being assigned a mission with Oliver Kirkham— that was *crazy*. The Seductors never pursued a target more than once. It was too dangerous.

I had finally gone insane. There was no doubt about it.

Yet, until I was released from lockdown, I knew that was all I was going to think about.

I had to pray my confinement wasn't going to last much longer. Four months was a really long time.

I needed to get out of here, and not just for my sanity. I needed to make sure my suspicions were wrong.

CHAPTER ONE

"At least try and crack a smile, Jade," Molly moaned as I threw my suitcase down on my bed. *Smile*! I'd just been called back to headquarters from a break in Hawaii as a matter of urgency. How could I be *happy* about that?

"Molly, I'm so pissed right now. I'm sick of looking at these damn walls. If Sonia is going to put me on lockdown again, I'll go insane." I was trying not to stress myself out, but months of confinement had taken its toll on me.

Never in my wildest dreams did I imagine Oliver would search for me as long as he did, but finally, after *six months* of every lead he followed being a dead end. He had admitted defeat and I was released from lockdown. I couldn't believe after only eight days away, I'd been called back, though.

"It could be a new mission," Molly mused, sitting on the edge of my bed.

"I hope so," I sighed, opening my suitcase and starting to unpack. If I was heading out on a mission soon, I'd need to sort out my laundry quickly.

"How was Hawaii until you were called back?"

"Good. I lay on the beach for a week, read a few books, and had a few cocktails. It was pure relaxation." I could feel Molly's eyes on me as I continued to go through my clothes. I wasn't in the mood for her questions today.

"Did you get it on with anyone?"

"No, I wasn't really away long enough." I snorted at her question. *Oh, Molly. She was never very subtle.* If it could only be that simple. I wasn't even sure how to move on from Oliver. He was all I could think about. In fact, I was still bringing myself to orgasm thinking about the way he touched my body. I knew that was pretty messed up after six months, but I doubted *any* man would ever wield the same power over me.

Having to get back on the saddle wasn't something I was looking forward to. This was the longest I'd ever gone without *physical* sex. I knew I had to get it over and done with eventually, though. Sex was part of my job, and holding onto something that was never going to happen wasn't going to help me move on.

"You know there are plenty of guys here that would be happy to help you out. I still think Miles has a soft spot for you," Molly grinned, nudging me playfully.

"Miles isn't my type. Not to mention, I'd probably scare the guy with my sexual appetite," I giggled, thinking about poor Miles. I'd had an eventful few months working for him in intelligence. He was an amazing guy, but just not my type at all.

"Aren't you horny, though?"

"Molly," I snorted. "If I want sex, I'll go and get it. Don't worry."

"Well, if Miss S brought you back for a mission, I'm sure you'll get some soon enough," she winked.

"We'll see," I mused, looking at my watch. I had almost an hour until I was due to see Sonia. Secretly, I was hoping this *was* about a mission. Taking on a new target was just what I needed.

"Are you still feeling down about you know who?"

I gawked at her. Did she really just ask about Oliver? How

the hell was that going to help me? "It's been over six months. I hardly think about him anymore," I lied, grabbing my laundry that needed to be washed.

"Uh huh, sure. Whatever you say." Molly eyed me as I walked past her. "Yeah, go and do your laundry rather than own up to your feelings. No wonder you're not over him yet."

I didn't respond. This was how I dealt with things. Okay, burying my head in the sand probably wasn't the best way to move on, but it was the only way I knew. It had worked these last six months, too.

"I heard you were back." I groaned internally as Mario spoke from behind me in the laundry room a little later. "Did Miss S put you on lockdown again?" he mocked.

"You're not funny, Mario." I didn't even look up at him as I continued to fold my clothes.

"I really thought I'd break you while you were cooped up in here. I was hoping you'd take your frustration out on me." By the level of his voice, I could tell that he was right behind me. I turned around quickly, pushing his chest before he laid a finger on me.

"How many times do I have to tell you, this isn't a game? I'm *not* fucking interested!" I seethed, barging past him. Mario grabbed my waist, trying to pull me toward him.

"Another few weeks and I would have had you. You wouldn't be a Seductor if you weren't addicted to sex like me. You're only holding back because you don't want to get attached. We'd be good together and you know it. I could give that sweet pussy of yours a real good beating if you just let go." I lost it, slamming the heel of my shoe hard into his foot. *Me* get attached to Mario's cock. I was wrong—this guy was hilarious. "Oww...

you fucking bitch!" he yelled, hopping around while clutching his injured foot. I didn't even try to hide my snigger as I walked past him. *You deserved that, Mario!*

I was still chuckling to myself when I bumped into Molly in the hallway.

"Sonia is ready to see you now." She had a worried look on her face.

"What's wrong?"

"Alicia came to get you."

"She's back? I thought she wasn't due back for a progress report for another few weeks." My mind was racing. Why the hell would Alicia come to get me? It didn't make any sense; Sonia knew I hated her.

"Sonia wanted her back early. I'm not sure things are going too well with the mission." Molly followed me back to my room. "What if your theory is right and Alicia has been with Oliver these last few months?" I dumped my clean clothes on my bed, trying to compose myself. I was making Molly paranoid now, and that wasn't good.

"Why would Oliver become a target again? It doesn't make any sense. You and Georgie have been telling me that for months."

"I don't know, but it all seems a little strange to me."

"You're really not helping. You're supposed to say that I've gone crazy. Do you know how ridiculous this all sounds?" I threw my arms up in the air in frustration.

"Go and see Miss S and finally put your mind at rest. Georgie and I know it's been eating away at you. You need answers, Jade."

"I can't hide anything from you two, can I?" I sighed,

grabbing my phone. Molly was right—I couldn't put it off any longer. I needed to find out what was going on.

* * *

Alicia was standing outside Sonia's office, talking on her phone when I arrived.

"No, really, it was me. I was clearly reading the signs wrong. I can't apologize enough." Alicia's eyes gleamed with smugness when she caught sight of me entering Sonia's office. What was all that about? "We'll forget it ever happened. I shouldn't have crossed my professional boundaries. I don't want this to come between us..." I didn't bother to listen to the rest of her conversation as my eyes caught Sonia.

"Jade," she said as she stood up from behind her desk. That was new. Sonia never stood up for anyone. "You can close the door." I closed it with a puzzled look on my face. "Alicia doesn't know I'm bringing you in on this mission yet." It *was* a mission! Thank God! No, wait...if Sonia was bringing me in, it could only mean one thing! *Damn it!*

"The mission involves working with *Alicia*," I groaned, taking a seat in front of her desk. "Don't get me wrong, I'm glad this *is* a mission, but do I have to work with her? Can't someone else do it?"

"Jade, I'm afraid you're our only hope. I'm about to go against everything I've ever done while running the Seductors, but I can't see any other way around it. Alicia has been on this case for almost two months and has gotten nowhere."

"You want me to take over Alicia's mission?" I frowned. Since when has Alicia had a problem seducing a man?

Everything started to dawn on me then, and I clutched the arms of my chair tightly.

"I need the two of you to work together. This steal... it's asking a lot. We aren't even sure if it exists." Now Sonia was losing me. "If we secure what we've been hired to find, our clients are willing to pay over one hundred million dollars. Maybe even more. There is no real price for it." I was sure my mouth fell to the floor. *One hundred million dollars?* What the hell was the steal? "Jade, I'm asking a lot of you here, but I've hit a wall. If Alicia can't work her magic, it can only mean one thing." With bated breath, I was hanging on her every word. "He isn't over you."

"Who isn't over me?" My mouth was so dry. I had to swallow my breath to stop my voice from trembling.

"Mr. Kirkham." *No!* This wasn't happening. The room began to spin. "The blueprints you stole are worthless without the power core, Jade."

"Power core?" I questioned, trying to wrap my head around everything. Oliver *was* Alicia's target. My suspicions had been right all along.

Had she just been speaking to him on the phone? I felt so light headed suddenly, and my stomach began to churn like I was going to throw up.

"It would seem Kirkham Industries may have found a new sustainable energy source for their weapons. If that's true, the world of nuclear weapons could change forever. Do you have any idea what price that information could bring us?"

"You're talking about nuclear weapons, Sonia. Isn't this mission too advanced for us?" I gasped, trying to catch my breath.

"That isn't any of your concern, Jade. Or mine. We do our job—no questions asked!"

"But it goes against Seductor policy to have the same target more than once. Oliver might not even want anything to do with me. I left him without an explanation."

"He'll forgive you when you admit your true feelings for him." No! That wasn't fair. She couldn't ask that of me. I couldn't leave him if he knew how I really felt. It would be too much. "It isn't a request either, Jade."

"Sonia, you don't know what you're asking of me."

"I know you fell in love with him, and I can't deny that I'm disappointed. I never thought you'd fall into that trap, but for once, we can use that to our advantage."

"I have no idea…"

"Don't try to bullshit me, Jade. I've been around too long for games," she interrupted sternly. "You *will* do this. If anyone can find that power core, it's you."

"What about Alicia? Where does she fit in?"

"Alicia is Mr. Kirkham's personal assistant."

"*What?*" I fumed. I could just imagine Alicia trying to seduce Oliver in his office, bending over his desk, making suggestive comments. I was livid!

"He's shown no interest in her whatsoever, Jade." That didn't make me feel any better. She'd been with him while I'd been stuck here.

"You should have given the mission to me in the first place," I glared, crossing my arms.

"I knew how involved you had become with Mr. Kirkham. I couldn't risk letting you near him and blowing your cover. You're the best Seductor I have."

"What's changed now?"

"I'm willing to make you an offer," she grinned, stretching to pick up a file from her drawer. "If you complete this mission, I'm willing to give you *this* life when your contract has been fulfilled." She pushed the file over to me and I opened it, gasping. I could take the identity of *Jade Gibbs* when I left the Seductors. The Jade Gibbs Oliver loved. Was she being serious?

"I don't understand…"

"Complete this mission and you can have Oliver back when your contract ends."

"You're serious?" Was this a trick? Would he even wait for me? How would I explain my disappearance for over four years? I was overthinking things, and I knew it.

"Yes, we can discuss the details once you've secured your place back at Mr. Kirkham's side. This offer is to be kept between the two of us, though. You know it goes against most Seductor rules, but this mission is unlike any we've had before."

"It won't be easy gaining his trust back," I admitted.

"This is going to be a long mission, Jade. You'll need time to infiltrate Mr. Kirkham's life and his family again. This isn't like the last mission. Alicia has already scanned all his files. There is no trace of this power core anywhere, so you'll need to earn his trust and pull the information out of him. You need to get right inside his life. You'll need to be by his side and watch every move he makes."

"How am I going to do that if he won't even speak to me? I ran out on him, Sonia! I can't picture him being that happy to see me again."

"He is still in love you with. You can use that as your advantage."

"It might not be enough."

"Brian Brentford is an old friend of Mr. Kirkham's. He's recruiting freelance interior designers for his new apartment buildings in New York." Sonia turned her laptop around for me to look at. The apartment buildings were impressive. Brian Brentford was a high-flying architect, so it didn't surprise me that he was friends with Oliver. "I've already secured you an interview in Washington on Thursday with Mr. Brentford. Once you've been hired, you'll be invited to the opening in New York which Mr. Kirkham will be attending. This will be your first contact with him. You will take residence in New York. I'm sure Mr. Kirkham won't be able to stay away from you when he learns you're living so close to him."

"When is the opening?" I was desperate to know how soon I'd see him.

"Two weeks from Friday." Two weeks? That wasn't long at all. "There is a lot of research for you to digest. I'd suggest you read Alicia's case notes, too. That will help you get up to speed with everything. I know you can do this, Jade, and I'm willing to reward you with your heart's desire if you can complete this mission."

"I accept, but I want your offer in writing," I replied. Right now, I'd agree to anything if it meant I got to see Oliver again.

"Agreed." Sonia stretched her hand out toward me, and we shook on it. "You can let Alicia in now."

"With pleasure," I smirked, getting up. This was going to be interesting.

Alicia was thankfully off her phone when I opened the door.

"Sonia is ready to see us both now," I called politely.

"*Both* of us?" She didn't seem very happy about that statement as she barged past me. "What is all of this about, Sonia?" I closed the door, rolling my eyes as I did. Working with Alicia was always so much fun—the 'waxing your bikini area' kind of fun.

"I'm bringing Jade in on this mission, Alicia," Sonia stated calmly.

"WHAT?!"

"You're no closer now than you were the day you started this mission. Mr. Kirkham isn't over Jade. That much is obvious."

"I'm working on him. He wants me, I can tell. If we hadn't been interrupted by his uncle in his office, he would have gone the whole way with me last week."

I took a deep breath before I spoke, but imagining her hands all over him clouded my mind. "Oliver doesn't date his employees, Alicia," I snarled. "You're wasting your time."

"Was I even talking to you?!" she yelled back.

"Alicia, I'm not impressed with your tantrum. Jade is joining this case whether you like it or not, and whoever gets Mr. Kirkham's heart first will lead the mission. You need to put aside your feud and work together." As she spoke, Sonia glared between both of us. Alicia and me working together? Yeah, that was *never* going to happen. "You both know what this assignment is worth. We need to report back with *something* to our client. They understand this steal will take some time, but we have yet to find out if it even exists."

"I won't let you down, Sonia. I'm willing to work together if Alicia is." It was a lie, of course. I didn't *need* Alicia's help, and I didn't want it. I knew Oliver better than she ever would.

"Thank you, Jade." Sonia turned to Alicia, waiting for her

response.

"I could have handled this, but if you want Jade on the mission, what else can I do?" she sulked, running her fake red nails through her hair.

"Excellent! Alicia, I want you to get Jade up to speed with everything. She leaves on Thursday for an interview with Mr. Brentford in Washington. Jade's first contact with Mr. Kirkham will be at the Brentford Apartments Opening in New York." Alicia simply nodded, but I could see that she was fuming inside. She knew I had the upper hand. Oliver might still be in love with me, after all. All I needed to do was gain his forgiveness. "That's everything for now. Jade, you'll need to pay Miles a visit to get your paperwork in order and to clear your back story for when you meet Mr. Kirkham again. He has secretly been trying to follow your every move. We need to make sure your story matches the destinations Miles faked to keep you safe."

"Thank you for believing in me, Sonia," I smiled, standing up. "I won't let you down."

"I have every faith in you. I'm glad to get you back out there."

"Don't mind the rest of us Seductors," Alicia muttered icily. "No one can match Jade."

"You could learn a few things from Jade, Alicia. She is a real professional. There are many reasons she is at the top of her game, and you'd be wise to try and follow them." Her words were truly touching. I never knew that was how Sonia saw me. I wasn't really the Jade she had just described anymore, though.

"I'll take my leave now and begin preparing for my interview in Washington." Sonia excused me with a nod and a small smile.

As I walked out of Sonia's office, I could hear Alicia raise her voice. She must have been furious at the turn of events. I knew she hated me as much as I hated her, but if working with her would give me Oliver, it was something I was willing to do.

I couldn't protect my heart this time, though. The moment I saw him, I knew I'd give him anything he wanted in return for his forgiveness.

If that *was* my heart—I'd give it to him gladly.

CHAPTER TWO

"Here are all your papers, Jade." Miles smiled sweetly at me. "Are you sure about all this?"

"I have no choice. Sonia needs me to take this mission."

"You want this mission too, don't you?" he questioned, handing me my fake passport. Why did it feel so good being Jade Gibbs again?

"Yes," I confessed with a sigh.

"Mr. Kirkham doesn't seem to want to give up on you, either. He did another background check yesterday to see if you'd used your account anywhere." Oliver was *still* looking for me. That was a good thing, right? "Did you get the information I sent you about your bank deposits?"

"Yes, I've studied them. I know where I've been these last six months."

"Make sure your tracker is working. I had issues with Georgie's earlier this week. It might be the software that I updated," he mused, going back to his computer.

"Don't I get any fancy gadgets to take with me?" I teased, leaning on his desk.

"There's no point until we know about this power core. You have your standard equipment, though."

"Do you think they're going too far with this steal?" I could confide in Miles. We became close in the months we'd worked together.

"Selling advanced nuclear weapons to the highest bidder? Yeah, I'd say they've outdone themselves this time. But we're all here to do a job, aren't we?" I nodded sadly. "Promise me you'll be careful."

"I always am."

"Mr. Kirkham has no idea about the stolen blueprints. We've advised our client to keep it all under wraps until we find out if this power core is even real."

"Do you think it could exist?"

"There have been so many advances in fission and fusion that it could be possible. By generating higher mission velocities with less reaction mass, it could be achieved. Kirkham Industries would need a higher energy density of nuclear reactions, though. That would take some creating." Miles had lost me already. "Sorry, Jade. It's my scientist head talking. I can see the glazed-over look in your eyes."

"You'd get along so well with Oliver," I giggled. "Does he really not know about the blueprints being stolen?"

"He's been too occupied with trying to find you, Jade. He has no idea that they were stolen, and I'll make sure he doesn't find out." Miles was amazing. He was all about keeping us Seductors safe.

"You're a real sweetheart," I beamed, pecking his cheek. He blushed bright red, like I knew he would.

"Who's going to keep you guys safe if I don't?" he mused, looking up from his computer screen.

"Sonia doesn't value you as much as she should."

"When you complete this mission, ask her for a pay raise for me, then," he chuckled.

"Deal," I smirked. "So, is this everything?"

"Yeah, good luck. Oh, I've downloaded information on Brian Brentford to help with your interview, too. I sent it to your phone so you can read it on the plane."

"That was very thoughtful."

"I do it for everyone." I knew that wasn't true, but I needed to get ready for my flight to Washington, so I didn't push it.

I was flying to New York immediately after my interview. I needed to secure myself an apartment, and had booked a room at The Peninsula, Manhattan while I visited a few real estate agents.

The opening for Brentford Apartments was at the St. Regis Hotel, which was just around the corner from The Peninsula. I needed a quick getaway if my first meeting with Oliver didn't go quite how I planned.

* * *

"I still think this mission involves him. I can tell by your face," Molly moped as I packed my bags.

"Shouldn't you be getting ready for *your* mission?" I pointed out, trying to change the subject. "You know I can't tell you. This mission doesn't concern you!"

"Why would he become your target again? Plus, do you really want to go there knowing Alicia has, too?"

"Molly, quit it, please!"

"I had to take some of his calls when he kept trying to reach you at your pretend office, Jade. I'm under no illusions about how he feels about you, and I know you're in love with him, too. I'm worried about you. How are you going to walk away after this? You had a hard enough time after the first mission."

"I'll be fine!" I threw my hand over my mouth, realizing my slip up.

"Are you for real?" Her eyes widened as her mouth went slack.

"You can't breathe a word of this—not even to Georgie or Drew. You know Sonia will come down on your ass hard!"

"Fucking hell, I'm speechless! Of course I won't say anything—I'm not stupid."

"I've got this, Molly. I'll be fine, I promise," I murmured, zipping my suitcase.

"Okay," she sighed, getting up. "You go and have more amazing sex with that hot target of yours. I'm not jealous in the slightest."

"It might take a while before we get to that. I have a feeling he's not going to be happy to see me."

"He's in love with you, Jade. You'll work it out. Just remember to look after this." She poked my chest. "Being in love with your target isn't a good place to be." I knew that, but Molly didn't know that I had the chance to be with Oliver when my contract was over—as long as he never found out I was a Seductor.

"I'm not in love with him. I'm just addicted to the way he fucks me," I lied.

"You can't fool me." I shook my head, giving Molly a tight hug goodbye. When I stepped back, I grabbed my suitcase and papers, and was finally on my way. It seemed surreal that in less than two weeks I would see Oliver again. The question was: would he be happy to see me?

* * *

I lay on one of the orange lounge chairs near the pool at The Peninsula, relaxing and soaking up the sun. I was trying to calm myself because today was opening day. In a matter of hours, I'd be face to face with Oliver, trying to explain my absence for the last six months.

My interview with Mr. Brentford had gone effortlessly in Washington, even if he had spent most of the time talking to my chest.

I had also managed to secure an apartment in Manhattan, not too far away from Oliver's stunning penthouse. Although, I had to wait a few weeks until I could move in.

I was hoping that by making myself easily accessible to him, he wouldn't be able to keep away.

He might not be able to stand the sight of me at first, though.

That was what worried me the most—Oliver's initial reaction. I'd hurt him, but would he be willing to forgive me?

"Jade?" I was snapped out of my thoughts by someone standing in front of me. I groaned to myself at the sight of Brian Brentford hovering over me. His eyes raked over every inch of my body. Only wearing a red bikini, I quickly pulled my robe around my body and sat up.

"Mr. Brentford, what are you doing here?" I acted shocked when really, I knew what his game was. He'd been trying to make a play for me from the moment I entered his interview room in Washington.

"Sorry to drop by unannounced, Jade." His eyes were lingering on my legs as he spoke. "Would you mind arriving a little earlier tonight to help me set up the room?" Great, that meant I had even less time to get ready now.

"Of course I can," I smiled, taking my sunglasses off. "I'd better get ready soon, then."

"Don't let me keep you. I thought I'd ask you in person since I was passing right by your hotel anyway. Can I take you to lunch tomorrow, too? The floor plans for the apartments you've been assigned have arrived. We could look at them over a shared meal." Oh, I had every hope that Oliver would save me and stake his claim by then. Lunch with Mr. Brentford sounded awful.

"Sure," I replied quietly. I still had to be shy, Jade Gibbs, when really, all I wanted to tell this asshole to take a hike. Just the way he was watching me was creeping me out.

Mr. Brentford wasn't much older than Oliver. I could only imagine what the rivalry was like between the two *friends.* It wasn't that I was planning on making Oliver jealous by using Mr. Brentford, but Alicia had been alone with him for two whole weeks. Who knew what schemes she'd played trying to seduce him. I only prayed Oliver hadn't fallen for her charms.

"I'll see you later then, Jade, and thank you." Mr Brentford left without another word.

I looked down at my watch, knowing I needed to make a move to get ready. I needed to look my best for tonight. Why was I suddenly feeling so worked up?

* * *

"Thank you for this, Jade," Mr. Brentford smiled as I began

to place leaflets around the tables. It was only the two of us and a few waitstaff in the room.

I'd gone for an elegant backless black dress tonight, with a slit that showed off my long legs. The cut of the dress was very low, so I'd taped my breasts in for extra support. I'd curled my hair, too, tying a few loose strands up. I hoped it was enough to impress Oliver tonight. I knew he wouldn't be happy to see me at first.

"It's my pleasure," I muttered, keeping a close eye on the door. Oliver was on his way. Alicia had already informed me that he'd left half an hour ago.

"I better go to reception and check if my guest speaker has arrived yet."

"Are you going to let me know who it is?" I giggled, moving around the table as I tried to get some distance from him. Mr. Brentford always had to stand so close to me. Men!

"Oh, I suppose it won't do any harm to tell you," he grinned, looking behind me. "Oh, wait! It doesn't matter now. You can actually meet him. He just walked in." I froze, scared to move. My back was facing the door, and as I placed the last leaflet down on the table, Mr. Brentford called out to him. "Oliver! I was just about to come to the reception to meet you. I have someone I want you to meet." I swallowed hard and slowly began to turn around.

"Don't worry about it, Brian. I'm early for once," Oliver chuckled. He was getting closer. Every nerve ending in my body intensified just from hearing his voice. It had been too long.

"This is Jade," Mr. Brentford commented as Oliver and I locked eyes.

The world around us seemed to slow. Christ, I could have

drowned in those dark, hooded brown eyes. Oliver looked good, really good. His hair was a little shorter, but his face hadn't changed at all. He perhaps looked more tired, but I couldn't even imagine what he'd been through in the last few months.

"O...Ol...Oliver," I whispered, forcing my words out.

"Jade?" His face was full of confusion and hurt. "Is this a joke? You turn up *now*? After all this time?"

"Let me explain," I pleaded, reaching for him.

"Don't!" he threatened, taking a step back. "You're wasting your breath! I'm not interested in *anything* you have to say. You made yourself clear six months ago." With that, he stormed off.

Ignoring Mr. Brentford's calls, I rushed after him. My body was moving of its own accord; I didn't even have to think about it.

I found him pacing the hallway with his face in his hands.

"Oliver, please," I whimpered. His eyes snapped up to me instantly, and I was frozen in place by his gaze as he began to stalk toward me. What was he going to do? I couldn't read his eyes. They looked half crazed.

"What the *fuck* is going on?" he seethed, pushing me up against the wall. "Where the hell have you been?" He pressed his hands either side of my head, holding me in place. I was breathing erratically from all the adrenaline pumping through my veins. Watching his lips, I longed to run my fingertips across them. I'd never wanted a man the way I wanted him. It was all-consuming. Every nerve ending in my body was pulsing for him.

"I...I was trying to build up the courage to see you," I muttered.

"You walked out on me! I confessed *everything* to you, and you fucking walked out!" He pushed off the wall, pulling at his hair.

"Oliver, I'm sorry. I..." I tried to reach for him, but he pulled back.

"What are you doing here, Jade? It makes no sense."

"I've come back to beg for your forgiveness. I'm sorry. You *have* to believe me."

"How can I *ever* trust you again? I opened my heart up to you and you walked out on me." The pain in his eyes paralyzed me. I'd done this to him.

"I'm moving to New York." He looked troubled by my confession. Six months ago, he would have been elated by that news.

"Why?" he snarled.

"Why do you think?" The sexual tension was beginning to build between us. "Give me a chance to explain, please?" I pleaded.

Oliver sighed deeply, closing his eyes for a short second. They were softer when he opened them again.

"I can't believe you're really here. I thought I'd never see you again." He moved his hand into my hair, twisting one of my curls around his fingers.

"I know you're angry with me, but please just hear me out. There are things you don't know about me."

"Jade..." He was obviously conflicted as he watched my lips. "I can't do this. I can't open up my world to you again knowing you could leave at any moment. It's too late, I..."

"I was going to come and see you; I promise. I didn't want to stay away as long as I did, but the longer I left it, the harder it became." His defenses were faltering; I could see it in his eyes. The hand that was in my hair moved to stroke the side of my face. "Give me a chance to explain, please," I pleaded, gripping his jacket and pulling him toward me. Our mouths were only inches apart now. Oliver licked his lips, gazing down at me.

I closed my eyes as he began to close the small distance between us. I wanted to drown in this kiss and never come back up for air.

As his lips brushed mine, I gasped, opening my mouth slightly to take in his kiss. Suddenly a voice interrupted us.

"Umm...Oliver?" I could never mistake Alicia's voice. I tried to control my fury as he backed away from me completely. "I decided to come after all," she smiled, looking stunning in her tight, red satin dress. *Damn her to hell!* This was supposed to be *my* first meet. She shouldn't even be here. Not to mention red was *my* color!

"Oh, what a lovely surprise," Oliver muttered, a little flustered. "You look beautiful, Alicia." My heart sank as I watched him walk over to greet her with a soft peck on the cheek. It didn't seem like a professional thing to do to me. Had he fallen for her charms?

"Who's your friend?" she asked, looking in my direction.

He gazed at me with sad eyes before speaking. "She's no one." I tried to stop the tears from stinging my eyes at his cold words. Was I really nothing to him?

"Well, I think the drinks reception is this way," Alicia smiled, pulling Oliver away from me. With one last glance in my direction, he let her lead him away.

* * *

"How do you know Oliver?" Mr. Brentford asked once I'd

joined him back in the now full ballroom. I picked up a glass of white wine that was offered to me by one of the waitstaff.

"It's a long story," I stressed, taking a large gulp of wine.

"Do you know him on a personal or professional level?" I widened my eyes at his question. "I'm sorry, that was rude of me. It's just…I've never seen Oliver react that way before."

"Have you been friends long?"

"Almost ten years," he replied, touching my arm. "Jade, if you need me to keep him away from you, I can. He can be a little intense."

"I'll be fine." I smiled shyly, pulling away from his touch. Oliver and Alicia walked in at that moment with fresh drinks in their hands. His gaze instantly fell upon me, and I began to burn as I watched the hunger in his eyes. I was sure it matched my own.

"Are you sure?"

"Yes," I muttered, walking away to network with a few of the guests.

* * *

I felt Oliver's eyes on me throughout the evening. Whenever I turned to look at him, I found him already watching me. He didn't make any attempt to talk to me, though. It seemed as if Alicia was keeping him on a tight leash.

I'd forgotten how much I loved watching him converse with people. Sitting at the bar for an hour, I observed him with four different groups of people. Everyone seemed to be in awe of him, and I could understand why. I'd fallen hard for the Oliver Kirkham charm myself.

"You aren't going to win this mission, Jade," Alicia whispered into my ear as she joined me at the bar.

"Oh, really?" I crossed my legs, turning to give her my full attention. This I couldn't wait to hear.

"I've *had* him, Jade," she goaded, running her hands through her fake hair. It took all my strength not to raise my hand up and slap her. That was what she wanted, though. She was trying to make me blow my cover. Jade Gibbs wouldn't confront anyone, let alone a stranger.

Okay, so Alicia might have slept with Oliver, but he wasn't in love with her. I'd left him months ago. He was a free man.

It didn't stop my heart from aching when I imagined the two of them together, though. "Give up now," she whispered as we both watched Oliver make his way over toward us with a slight frown on his face.

"Never," I muttered before he reached us.

CHAPTER THREE

"I was just asking Jade how you two knew each other," Alicia stated as Oliver handed her a fresh glass of wine.

"Jade is an acquaintance of mine." His tone was indifferent. He didn't even look in my direction as he spoke. Was that really all I was to him now?

"Really? It looked like you were more than that outside," she giggled into her wine glass. She was enjoying this, I could tell.

"I have no idea what you mean," he muttered.

"If you'll excuse me," I sighed, standing up. I wasn't going to sit here for Alicia's amusement.

"Don't leave on my account... What was your name again?" she asked with an almost sickening smugness.

"Jade," I snapped, starting to move. "It was nice to see you again, Oliver," I whispered, not meeting his eyes. He moved closer toward me, which meant I had to brush past him to leave. I held in a groan when I felt his hand on my bare back as I walked past. How could one simple touch ignite so much inside me?

I quickly joined the closest group of people I could find. A few of them were interior designers that I would be working with here in New York, which made it easy to fit right in. I tried to focus on my conversation with them, but my eyes kept wandering the room, trying to find Oliver.

"Have you been in this business long?" a tall, dark, and extremely tanned man asked me.

"About five years," I muttered as Oliver came into view again. It looked as if he was heading toward me.

"What area do you specialize in?"

"Artwork, mainly."

"Miss Gibbs helped me purchase a couple pieces of artwork a few months ago," Oliver called from behind me. The whole group began to fall over themselves simply because Oliver Kirkham joined in our conversation. "She did, however, leave the design on my office unfinished."

"You never actually agreed to any of the designs, Mr. Kirkham," I countered, quirking my eyebrow at him. He tried to hide the amusement in his eyes. What? Now he was talking to me. Why?

He stood close to me while the group began to quiz him about his life. Alicia was nowhere to be seen. Had he asked her to leave?

"Are you talking to me now?" I whispered when we were finally alone a little later.

"Yes." His tone was still guarded.

"Does this mean you're going to give me a chance to explain?"

"I'm thinking about it," he sighed, looking into the crowd.

"You've hardly let me out of your sight all evening."

"That's because I keep thinking you're a dream. Jade, I've been looking for you for the last six months."

"Looking for me?" I frowned, playing my cover.

"Don't be mad," he winced. "I put a tracker on your back account."

"You did *what*?!" I fumed. Any normal woman wouldn't be happy with that confession. For me, however, it showed he still cared.

"I'm sorry, but I needed to know you were safe. Jade, you disappeared into thin air. Can you really blame me?"

"That is my personal life, Oliver! You had no right to interfere! Have you been tracking me this whole time?" We were in the far corner of the room, but I was drawing attention to us because of my outburst.

"Are you really giving me a hard time about this?" he snarled back with cold eyes. "I thought you might have been kidnaped. My job makes anyone I care about a target. I had to be sure you were okay. You did far worse, Jade, and you know it!"

"You're judging me before you even know the whole story."

"I opened my world up to you, and you threw it in my face. I have a right to be pissed about it!" He was becoming more enraged as we spoke. "Do you have any idea how hard it's been for me? My business even suffered while I was trying to find you."

"I didn't mean…"

"Why did you leave me, Jade? I need to know." I was about to answer him when Mr. Brentford joined us.

"Oliver, we're almost ready for you now," he smiled, looking over at me. "You're not monopolizing Jade, are you?"

"We were just catching up, Mr. Brentford." I smiled weakly, looking up at Oliver who appeared to be angry at his friend's interruption.

"Well, I still think you've taken enough of Jade's time. Let's get you set up on stage," Mr. Brentford teased, patting him on the back.

"We *will* finish this later," Oliver muttered in my ear, running his hand down my bare back before making his way to the front of the room.

He was quite the motivational speaker. Oliver must have been on stage for at least an hour, answering questions after his speech.

Alicia returned not long after he had gotten onstage, but luckily, she didn't approach me again.

"Are we still okay for lunch tomorrow?" Mr. Brentford asked while I was at the bar waiting for a drink. Oh, crap! How was I going to get out of that?

The evening was winding down now, and Oliver was deep in conversation with a large group of people in the far corner of the room.

"Oh, I...I..."

"I'll pick you up at your hotel at noon. I thought we could try a new Italian restaurant in Brooklyn." He wasn't taking no for an answer, so I simply nodded. As I gazed into the crowd, I noticed Oliver watching me. "Jade..." Mr. Brentford stroked my arm, pulling my eyes away from Oliver. "I'd really love an opportunity to get to know you." He traced his hand down my arm, making his way toward my back. "Mm...you have very soft skin," he mused, stroking my bare back. Already pinned up against the bar, I couldn't move. This creep needed to learn to keep his hands to himself. I pushed his chest back, counting to five inside my head as I worked at calming my rage. He was lucky I had to stay in character. I was ready to floor him if his hands got any lower.

"If you'll excuse me," I replied awkwardly, breaking free

from his hold.

I decided to go outside for some fresh air when I saw Alicia laughing with Oliver. Her hand was pressed to his chest while the group they were in chuckled along with them.

Why did it feel as if this mission was slipping from my hands already?

I took three deep breaths, gripping the wall in front of me.

"Here you are," a soft voice called. I turned to see Oliver making his way over to me.

"Sorry, I needed some fresh air." I smiled shyly, wrapping my arms around myself. That was the typical Jade Gibbs body language. It would help me look vulnerable. I needed him to want to take care of me like before. I needed to be back inside his world, and *not* just for this mission.

"Are you cold?" he asked in concern, slipping out of his jacket.

"Not really," I muttered as he moved to drape his jacket over my shoulders. We stood there staring into each other's eyes for a few short moments, his hands still on my shoulders. He seemed to be searching for something and was hesitant to let me go.

"I thought you were going to make another run for it," he finally admitted in a whisper. "I came outside to stop you."

"I'm not running anywhere," I sighed, pulling his jacket tighter around my body as he finally let me go.

"How do I know that? I didn't think you'd run the first time."

"You seem to have done fine without me. The woman in the red dress seems *nice*."

"*Alicia?*" he frowned. "She's my PA."

"So, you've changed your rule about dating employees?"

"Jade, I have no idea what you're trying to imply." His tone was becoming annoyed again, but I needed to know if Alicia had seduced him. Deep down, I was sure he wouldn't fall for her charms, but I needed to hear it from him. "Well, fine. If we're going to have this kind of conversation right now, I don't like the fact that you're working for Brian. He's a sexual predator, Jade. His hands have been all over you tonight!" Wow! Where the *hell* did that come from?

"Are you trying to imply that I can't protect myself?" I fumed. "Believe it or not, I was fine until *you* walked into my life!" I was breaking character a little, but I was angry that he thought I could be that naive.

"Why did you come back to New York, Jade? You should have just kept running!"

"Maybe I will!" I yelled, standing up. His jacket slipped off my shoulders as I rose. I had no idea why I was losing it so much, but I couldn't stop.

"Do you run from everyone you love?" His words struck me down like a bolt of lightning, and I fought back the images from my past. Now wasn't the time to be thinking about the people I had loved and let down. Unfortunately for Oliver, he'd sparked a pure rage that had been dormant inside me for a long time.

"What gives you the right to ask me that?" I screeched. Startled, he took a step back at my sudden advance. "You're the one who decided to wear your heart on your sleeve! I told you not to put your trust in me. I *warned* you. I'm damaged, Oliver. You should have stayed away!"

"Jade," he soothed, trying to reach for me. "Calm down."

"No! You think you know me, but you don't!" Without really thinking, I started to storm off down an alley. I needed to breathe. I was so angry.

"Jade," Oliver called as he followed me, "you were the one who walked out on me, remember?"

I stopped in my tracks and spun around to face him. "You had to complicate everything! Why couldn't it have just been about the sex?"

"It meant more to you than sex. I *know* it did." With each step he took, he closed the distance between us, and my body began to burn. "Why do you fight it?" he asked, backing me up against the wall.

"Why do you look too closely and complicate everything? What happened to taking things slow?" I countered.

"I couldn't help the way I felt. I wanted you—only you."

"You should never let emotions get the better of you."

"So, you're trying to tell me it was only about sex to you? Nothing more?" he muttered, slipping his hands inside my dress softly rubbing my thighs. Jesus, my body was in spasms, igniting all the memories of how he made me feel.

"You know I care about you." My words must have sparked a rage inside him, because I felt him grab both my legs and hold me against the wall. "Are you going to take me right here in this alley?"

"Don't tempt me, Jade. I'm so angry right now. It won't be pretty if I lose control."

"I want you to," I yearned, squeezing him between my legs. Our closeness seemed to have an effect on him, and I felt him grip me tighter. I could feel his erection growing against my stomach. "Please, Oliver, take me. My body is burning for you."

He gave in with a groan, beginning to kiss and suck down my neck. It wasn't enough, though. I needed to feel his lips on mine.

"Ugh, Jade, what are you doing to me?" His hands were snaking up my body toward my breasts.

"Stop thinking about it. Just go with your feelings," I purred, moving my fingertips over the top of his dress pants.

He froze with his lips still pressed to my neck. "Now you're bringing *feelings* into this?" he seethed, his mouth brushing against my skin as he spoke. *Shit!* I'd said the wrong thing, but when he was this close, I had a habit of losing my mind. "You're contradicting yourself. How am I supposed to keep up?"

"I...I..." I had no answer for him.

"I can't do this, Jade. Not anymore," he winced, pulling away from me.

"You can, just..."

"No! This isn't going to go anywhere. You made your *feelings* very clear when you walked out on me six months ago. I'm not looking for sex. I need more. Did you have any intention of coming to see me? Or was this meeting strictly by chance?"

"Yes, I was going to come see you, I just needed to gather the courage."

"I don't believe you," he sighed, looking away from me.

"If you won't let me, explain, I can't prove you wrong."

"Maybe I don't want you to prove me wrong." His words were ice cold and they sliced me in two. He didn't want me anymore. Was that what he was trying to tell me?

He stood motionless, watching me. I had no idea what was going on in that head of his.

"Oh." I shrank back slightly, wrapping my arms around

my body as I tried to hold myself together. "I understand. I shouldn't have come back, I get it. You've moved on. I'm sorry for wasting your time," I whimpered, squeezing past him and making my way back inside.

He didn't follow after me like I hoped.

I didn't want to be at this opening a moment longer. Spotting Mr. Brentford in the distance, I made my way over to him. "I'm not feeling too well, Mr. Brentford. I hope you don't mind, but I'm going to go back to my hotel."

"Oh, Jade, let me escort you." I was going to refuse until I saw Oliver making his way back into the room. His eyes were searching for someone.

"Are you sure you don't mind?" I smiled sweetly.

"Of course not. We'll take my car. It will get you home quicker. Do you have a coat?" I nodded as Oliver made his way over to us.

"Jade, wait please," he pleaded.

"This will have to wait, Oliver. Jade isn't feeling very well, so I'm taking her back to her hotel. If you need to speak with her for some reason, you can contact my office tomorrow," Mr. Brentford said harshly.

"Jade, I...I..." Oliver couldn't finish his words, so I looked down at the floor as his friend escorted me away.

"Did you need any help up to your room?" Mr. Brentford asked when we arrived at the hotel. *Oh, there was no way he was coming anywhere near my room.*

"No but thank you for escorting me."

"I hope you're feeling better by our lunch date tomorrow, Jade," he called as I began to leave.

"I hope so, too. Thank you." I smiled shyly, making my way

to the elevator. *What a moron.*

I collapsed onto my bed, exhausted. Tonight, hadn't gone quite how I'd planned, and it was draining.

It wasn't like I was expecting to walk right back onto Oliver's bed, but had he really given up on me? Why was he still looking for me, then? None of it made any sense.

Sonia messaged for a progress report not long after I got back. I was typing up my response while listening to some soft rock music when a knock came at my door.

My heart began to hammer loud in my chest. Had he come to apologize?

"What the hell did you do to Oliver? The guy looks like he's in pain," Alicia snapped, pushing her way inside. *Great!* She was the one person I *didn't* want to see again tonight.

"I have no idea what you mean," I spat back. "And I didn't invite you into my room!"

"Look, Jade, we're on this mission together whether we like it or not!"

"I'm not working with you on this mission, Alicia. Oliver is *my* target! You shouldn't have even been there tonight. It was my first contact!"

"Technically, I think you'll find he's mine. I'm the one sharing a bed with him."

"I don't believe you," I snarled. "Oliver denied that when I asked him."

"Of course, he would. He doesn't date employees. Face it, Jade, you've already lost. Oliver is almost *mine,* and there is nothing you can do about it. I'll have that power core in no time and finally be able to knock you off your pedestal. I have no idea what Sonia sees in you, anyway." Oh, if Alicia wanted to war, she

45

had one. I was far from done with this mission. In fact, I'd only just started.

"Why are you even here, Alicia? What if Oliver found out you came here to see me? How would you explain that?"

"He's gone back to his apartment. There is no chance of him finding out. I came here to tell you to give up. He's not interested in you anymore."

"You're wrong. He's mad at me now, but he loves me. I can still feel the connection we share."

"I intend to break it. Do you think I've forgotten what you did last year?"

"I'm not backing down on that. You overstepped the rules, and I couldn't let you do it."

"You better watch you back, Jade. I'll bring you down this time. One way or another, I'll make you pay."

"Threats don't scare me," I glared. "There is nothing you can use to get to me." Only Oliver could be used against me, but Alicia didn't know that.

"Oh, I'll find something."

"It's time for you to leave. You've overstayed your welcome." I marched over to my door, holding it open for her.

"I'll be watching you, Jade."

"And I'll be doing the same with you. You haven't won yet, Alicia. Not by a long shot."

"We'll see," she smirked, strutting off down the hallway.

My heart was racing so fast. Oliver wouldn't pick Alicia over me; I was sure of it. So why was there doubt in the back of my mind?

CHAPTER FOUR

I didn't really want to make an effort for my lunch date with Mr. Brentford, but he was the only thing linking me to Oliver at the moment.

Reluctantly, I opted for a sophisticated, red cocktail dress. It wasn't very revealing, but it did fit my body like a glove. I didn't do much with my hair, though. My natural, loose curl was enough to finish off the look. In my mind, there was no reason to put in the extra effort. It wasn't like I was trying to impress my *boss*.

Mr. Brentford was already waiting for me when I arrived at reception. *Talk about enthusiastic!*

"Wow, Jade, you look stunning," he beamed, kissing my cheek and hugging me. His hands were too low on my back as he escorted me out of the hotel, and I had to take a deep breath to maintain my composure. "How are you feeling today?"

"Much better, thank you," I smiled, allowing him to lead me outside.

"I thought we'd take my limo." What was it about rich men that made them use their wealth to seduce a woman?

"You didn't have to go to so much trouble," I murmured, watching him as he joined me in the backseat.

"You seem to be a woman who enjoys the finer things in life." He pulled out a bottle of wine as he spoke. How cliche could this guy get? "Would you care for a glass of wine?"

"I better not. My stomach is still a little woozy from yesterday," I winced, moving further down the seat to get some room. Why did he insist on being so close to me all the time?

The new Italian restaurant he took me to was very modern. Most of the large space was white except for a deep purple feature wall and tiny twinkle lights that covered the entire ceiling. The kitchen was an open layout, and all the chefs were busy preparing food for the bustling lunch service.

Mr. Brentford helped me into my chair in the far corner of the restaurant before finally taking a seat with his back to the whole room.

"This place has had some great reviews already," he mumbled, picking up the menu to look over. The sommelier took our orders while we were still deciding what to eat.

"Are you having an antipasto?"

"Mm...I was just going to have a main dish." He smiled and nodded while looking back at his menu. "You didn't need to go to all this trouble for a business lunch, Mr. Brentford."

"Please, call me Brian, Jade."

"Sorry, *Brian*," I giggled as someone in the distance walked in and caught my eye. *No, it couldn't be.* Why would Oliver be having lunch here?

As the person drew closer, I gasped. It *was* Oliver, and he was scanning the crowd. I sank down into my chair, trying to hide myself from his view. What were the odds of him being here?

"Jade, are you okay?" Brian frowned, looking at me over his menu.

"I...um...Oliver just walked in," I muttered, gazing toward

him. It was bad timing, because as I did, Oliver's eyes locked with mine. Anger seemed to cross his face for a short second when he noticed Brian sitting opposite me.

"Why is he here? Did you invite him?" Brian fumed.

"No, I have no idea what he's doing here."

"Are you going to explain what's going on between the two of you? This is getting ridiculous, Jade. You are *my* employee. He already attempted to warn me off you last night when I came back from taking you to the hotel."

"He did what?" I gasped, watching Oliver make his way to a table a few feet from ours. He wasn't even going to come over and say hello? Was he meeting someone here?

"Are you in some kind of relationship with him? I need to know!"

"I don't know what I am to him anymore." I looked over at Oliver, who was already sipping a glass of water, gazing directly at me.

"Try to ignore him. We're here on a business lunch, and he's being a cocky bastard. That's his style. Trust me, you're better off not getting involved with him."

"Maybe he has a meeting here, too?"

"I doubt it. I don't think he's here by chance. Is he with anyone now?" Stretching in my seat to see around Brian, I made sure no one was at Oliver's table. He was talking to the waiter and didn't notice.

"No, he's alone," I breathed.

"Pay no attention to him. He wants you to make a big deal out of this. Ignore him," he replied sharply, clearly annoyed. *Ignore Oliver?* That wasn't going to be easy.

I almost made it through my lunch without any eye

contact with him. Brian and I made the best of our time and talked business. He loved my ideas of showcasing one of the apartments as an art gallery.

He also tried to show off with his knowledge of wine, sending three bottles back that he believed had been corked, or not stored properly.

"I'm sorry, Madam." A waiter placed a bottle of lager down in front of me while I watched Brian taste his fourth bottle of wine. "This is from Mr. Kirkham. He said he thought you might be more comfortable drinking this." *Damn, I loved him!* I snorted, covering my mouth as Brian frowned at the bottle.

"I'm sorry, Brian. It's an inside joke," I giggled. Oliver smirked at me as I glanced at him.

"I didn't have you down as a beer drinker, Jade."

"Mmhmm," I muttered, not really paying any attention to him. Oliver was becoming *very* distracting.

"If you want to finish the meal at his table, Jade, just say so," Brian sulked, throwing his napkin down on the table. "You've hardly kept your eyes off him since he arrived."

"I'm sorry. It's just that Oliver and I have issues we need to resolve."

"Go to him. We can finish this conversation in my office on Monday."

"Are you sure?" I knew he was angry, but I didn't care right then.

"Go," he fumed. "I'll settle up and come say goodbye at his table." I didn't need to be told twice.

Oliver's eyes were fixed on me as I slowly got up and stalked toward him, bringing my bottle of lager with me. I used a slow, sexy sway of my hips to draw him in further. He subconsciously licked his lips as his eyes wandered over my body. The red dress I was wearing showed off all my curves. I could read the want in his eyes. His desire for me hadn't diminished.

"Oliver, what are you doing here?" I asked, standing in front of him.

"Please take a seat, Jade," he smirked. I couldn't deny this man anything.

"I'm still angry with you," I sulked, sitting down and crossing my arms. "I'm on a business meeting for Christ's sake!"

"Judging the way Brian has been looking at you, I can assure you business was the furthest thing from his mind. He's trying to make you another notch on his bedpost!"

"Why would you even care if that was true?" I snapped coldly.

"Sorry about the way I acted last night. I was angry and confused." His voice was speaking right to my center. "Have you forgotten that you walked out on me six months ago? Now suddenly you're back. How the hell am I supposed to react to that?"

"How many times do you want me to apologize?"

"I need more than an apology if we try to make *this* work again."

"Tell me what I need to do," I pleaded, leaning closer to him. "I'll do anything."

"I'm the kind of guy who needs trust. That is the one thing you can't give me, Jade—not anymore."

"Then why are you even talking to me?" He studied my face for a minute, and my chest became tight as my heart began to beat furiously from all the adrenaline. Why was I suddenly feeling so hot?

"You have a hold on me I can't explain." His eyes darted behind me. "I'm sorry to monopolize Jade, Brian," he muttered, still looking at me.

"I'm sure you are, Oliver," Brian fumed, glaring at him. "I'll see you in my office at nine a.m., Jade. We can finalize your drafts then."

"Thank you, Mr....I mean Brian," I rebuffed.

"Have a wonderful afternoon, Jade." With that, Mr. Brentford left.

"He's pissed at me," Oliver chuckled, watching him leave.

"Of course he is. We were on a *business lunch*!"

"Did you want dessert?" he asked, picking up the menu while completely ignoring my last comment. I wanted something but it wasn't food, and I was sure he could read my face. He licked his lips and tilted his head, causing a gush of wetness between my legs.

"Only if you're having something," I managed to force out with a blush. It was amazing how easily I could go back to shy Jade. Maybe it was because I loved the way Oliver looked at *that* Jade—like he wanted to ride in on a white horse and save her. He had no idea just how past that I was, though. I could never be saved.

"Something tells me you're not thinking about dessert right now," he mused, raising his eyebrow at me. "I see some things haven't changed between us. I've never felt a sexual attraction like this before."

"You always have to bring everything back to sex, don't you?"

"You were the one asking me to take you against the wall

last night," he quipped with a gleam in his eyes.

"Then you told me I should have kept on running!" I glared, raising my voice slightly.

"Let's not do this here," he winced. "Do you want dessert or not?" Was he still talking about food? I was completely lost.

"Why don't we share one? I'm not that hungry." Oliver nodded in agreement.

We quickly decided on the rich, chocolate mousse trio, and he ordered two more lagers while we waited.

"Brian didn't see the funny side of your joke with the lager," I giggled, playing with the empty bottle in front of me.

"I couldn't resist. Sitting here, watching your face as he tried wine after wine—I could tell how bored you were."

"You know me rather well."

"Not *that* well," he sighed, playing with his napkin. It wasn't like Oliver to be restless. "Why did you leave me that night in Macon?" *Whoa!* We were doing this right now?

"Everything was happening so fast. I felt suffocated."

"You could have told me. Why run? Was I really that bad?"

"Oliver, you hardly knew me and were declaring your love for me. You must see how frightening that is for a woman like me. I had no idea what you saw in me. What could someone like me really offer you? You're this high-flying businessman who meets with world leaders and makes some kind of nuclear machine. How can someone like me fit into your world?"

"You would have fit perfectly, Jade," he murmured, his voice as soft as velvet. There went another pair of panties.

"How can you know that?"

"You gave me a life outside of my job. No one has ever done that for me before. My desire for you was the best kind of distraction. It calmed me. I wasn't thinking about work twenty-four-seven." He always had a way of speaking straight to my heart. I was elated that I could make him feel that way. "I know you fell for me, too. What I want to know is why you fought it? Why did you leave?"

"I can't do this right now," I sighed, putting my face in my hands. I knew Sonia wanted me to use my real feelings for Oliver to trap him, but I wasn't prepared to do that just yet. Firstly, I needed to make sure she'd keep to her word about giving me the Jade Gibbs identity when my contract was up.

"Then when? Jade, you owe me answers."

"I know I do, but there is no easy answer."

"Is this about your ex, Mario?" *Ugh*! Why did he always have to bring Mario up when we argued?

"No, it's bigger than that," I sighed, watching as the waiter delivered our dessert.

The chocolate mousse looked delicious with its three layers of different chocolates topped with a ripe strawberry.

"Are we going to fight for the strawberry?" I grinned, picking up my spoon as he moved the decadent dish between us so we could share.

"Jade, I'm nothing but a true gentleman. The strawberry is all yours," he smirked, gazing at me with those dark orbs of his. It was difficult to control the need inside me. After all, I knew how well he could play with my body. I noticed the slight stubble on his chin and imagined how it would feel as it grazed the inside of my thigh. *Oh, God! Oliver between my legs while his tongue attacked my heated center...* I wanted him so much it was almost painful. It was a deep yearning in the pit of my stomach.

I smiled at him, picking the strawberry up with my fingers

before gently licking the chocolate mousse off it. His eyes turned hooded, watching my lips.

"I know what you're trying to do, Jade," he muttered, swallowing hard.

"I have no idea what you mean," I purred, sucking the strawberry into my mouth.

"Jesus, how can you be so innocent and sexy at the same time?" he stressed, taking a spoonful of mousse.

"I'm just eating some fruit," I teased. "What's so sexy about that?"

"Just eat the damn dessert, Jade," he pleaded with a slight smirk. I was breaking down his defenses, I could tell. All I needed was some time to make him realize that I wasn't going anywhere. Well, for the time being anyway. I couldn't think about completing this mission and having to leave him again. I only prayed that knowing I would be allowed back into his life once my contract was up would be enough to get me through.

The dessert was delicious. I couldn't stop my low moans as I took my last mouthful. Oliver looked a little uncomfortable as he sat in his chair watching me.

"Are you having that last bite?" I asked him, licking my lips.

"I'd rather watch you eat it," he murmured, leaning closer over the table. "Or better yet, why don't I feed it to you?"

"Mmm..." I purred, leaning in as he scooped the last bite of mousse from the glass. His eyes were fixated on my mouth as I wrapped my lips around his spoon.

"Oh, Jade," he whispered, playing with a loose strand of my hair once he'd put his silverware down. "What are you doing to me?"

"I'm not giving up on you, Oliver. If you need me to prove I'm not going anywhere, then I will. You just have to give me the chance." I stretched my hand across the table, entwining our fingers.

"I can't go through losing you again. I won't put my heart on the line like before, Jade." The torture in his voice was pure agony for me.

"I'm not asking you to," I soothed. "I'm asking you to give me a chance to make it up to you. I'm not asking for anything, just a few dates when you can fit me into your schedule."

"*Dates*?" he chuckled.

"I know we skipped that part before. If you want to know everything about me, I need time, too. There is a lot you don't know that's difficult for me to talk about. Can't we get to know each other first this time?"

"I wish I was strong enough to tell you no, but knowing that you're here in New York, I won't be able to keep away."

"Is that your way of saying yes?"

"Yes," he whispered, squeezing my hand that was still in his. "I'm willing to let you try and make it up to me." Oh, if only Oliver knew the real me. I could think of a few ways to make it up to him, and they all included riding his impressive cock. *Stop thinking about sex, Jade*. I had a long way to go until any of that could happen.

"Thank you," I beamed, closing my eyes for a short second.

"I need to be in a meeting soon. Can I give you a lift somewhere?"

"Oh, I'm staying at The Peninsula, but only for another week or so. Then I'll be moving into my new apartment."

"Where is your apartment?" he asked, signaling to the

waiter for the bill.

"Oh, um…it's on St. Andrew's Avenue," I blushed, playing with my empty bottle of lager.

"Is that so?" he mused, trying to hide his smirk. "Is that a coincidence that St Andrew's Avenue is only a few blocks from my penthouse?"

"Not really," I admitted, biting my lip. "I wanted to be close to you."

"I'm starting to see that now," he grinned, giving his card to the waiter to settle the bill.

"Come on. We better go before I'm late for my meeting." Oliver got up to help me out of my chair a few moments later. "Do you have a coat?" I nodded, noticing one of the waiters already making his way over with it.

I had to suppress a groan as Oliver helped me into my jacket and his hands lingered on my neck. The warmth of his touch was unlike anything I'd ever experienced before. It was beyond sexual. It went deeper than that, as if I could feel myself breaking apart piece by piece for this man. I was his in every single way, and for the first time in my life, I wasn't afraid to admit how much I needed someone.

"Are you ready?" he asked softly. I nodded, allowing him to lead me out of the restaurant.

"Why *did* you come to the restaurant?" I asked as we were waiting for the limo to pull around.

"I meant what I said about Brian, Jade. You need to be careful around him."

"You came just to keep an eye on me?" I gasped.

"Yes."

"Do you really think I'm that stupid?" I snapped, crossing

my arms.

"No, but Brian already sees you as a conquest. It's always been about rivalry between us. I came here to look out for you mostly. I certainly wasn't going to let him take you home again like last night!" My heart was beating so fast at his confession. Oliver still cared a great deal for me; that much was clear.

"I can take care of myself, you know," I beamed, nudging him playfully. "But thank you for looking out for me."

"It's my pleasure, Jade." The atmosphere became electric around us suddenly. Oliver was gazing down at my mouth, and subconsciously, I began to lean up toward him. I couldn't stop myself. I needed him too much.

"This is a bad idea, Jade," he muttered as my lips grazed his. Just as I was about to run my hands into his hair, the limo pulled up. "Saved by the limo," he chuckled against my mouth before pulling back. *He wasn't funny!*

"The limo never stopped us before," I purred with a seductive smile on my face. As I stepped into the backseat, I made sure he had a good view of my legs.

"A lot's changed since then," he pointed out, joining me. His eyes zoomed in on my legs, and I watched as they traveled all the way up toward my thighs. *Mm...and some things haven't, Oliver.*

"I know," I smiled sadly. "I have to earn your trust back. I get it."

"You understand why, don't you? This isn't just about me. I welcomed you into my family, Jade, and I didn't make that decision lightly. In my line of work, it's all about trust."

"I get it," I sighed, looking out the window.

"There wasn't anyone else while you were gone, by the

way," he whispered, making me snap my head around to look at him. Was he lying? Or was Alicia? "What?" he asked, studying my face.

"It's nothing," I mumbled, looking back out the window.

"No, there is something. I know that look, Jade. What's on your mind? I'm telling you the truth. There hasn't been anyone else. To be honest, I didn't have the time. I was too busy looking for you."

"You've really been looking for me all this time?" I gasped.

"Yes," he whispered, running his hand through my hair lovingly.

"What happened to your PA, Abigail?"

"Oh," he snorted, shaking his head at me. "This is about Alicia, isn't it?"

"I don't like her!"

"Jade, you don't even know her," he chuckled. "She is very good at her job. Actually, she's the best PA I've ever had." Oh, yes I did! I knew her better than Oliver did!

"Is that because she goes above and beyond her duties?" I sneered.

"I don't date employees and you know that!" he glared. Damn! Angry Oliver was drenching my panties again.

"I wasn't implying anything; I'm just telling you that I don't like her."

"Well luckily, you don't have to work with her." He could be such a cocky asshole sometimes. Why did I love that so much? It was probably because I knew how well he'd get along with the real Jade.

The limo came to a stop outside my hotel.

"Thank you for the ride," I smiled, sliding in my seat

toward the door.

"You're welcome," Oliver replied softly, watching me.

"So...you'll call me when you're free?" I asked, turning toward him as the driver opened the door for me.

"Yes, Jade, I will," he smiled, leaning in to peck my cheek. His hands dug into my back, pulling me against his chest. "I'll see you soon."

"Bye, Oliver," I whispered, stepping out of the limo a little unsteadily.

"Jade," he called with the window down. "Do you have a new cell number?" I nodded with a grin. "Can I have it?" With a smirk, I took a piece of paper out of my bag and wrote my number down for him. "Start thinking about a few restaurants you'd like to try," he muttered as I handed him the slip of paper. "And promise me you'll be careful around Brian."

"I promise," I sighed with a snigger. "Now go before you're late for your meeting."

Oliver nodded, closing the window as the limo began to drive off. Even through the black glass, I knew he was watching me until I was no longer in view.

All I had to do now was gain his trust back. Then I could start on the actual mission. I was going to make sure Alicia didn't get anywhere near this assignment.

CHAPTER FIVE

"These are all the contacts I've collected so far," Alicia sulked, throwing the paperwork down on my bed. "I haven't been able to gather any evidence to suggest even one of these scientists are working with Oliver on the power core, though."

"Have you checked the main hard drive in Macon?" I asked, flipping through the paperwork.

"Yes. Oliver took me there last month." So, I wasn't the only woman Oliver had taken there anymore. "There was nothing there unless he had any encoded files. But they would be unbreachable."

"Did you check with Miles? He would have found a way to infiltrate those files if they existed."

"I've asked him. I'm not an idiot, Jade. I've been on this case longer than you!"

"Yeah, and you've gotten nowhere, which is why Sonia called me in."

"You think you've won just because Oliver is taking you out for dinner on Friday. Well, he hasn't told you about the two week trip to Russia he and I are going on, has he?" *Ugh!* I hated this woman so much. How could she ignite so much jealousy inside me? "Oliver and me...alone for two weeks. I bet he's got a lot of pent up sexual frustration now that you're back. You might have done me a favor."

"You haven't slept with him yet, have you?" I yelled, holding myself back so I didn't smack her smug face.

"I said it to piss you off," she goaded with a grin. "I think you have a little soft spot for Mr. Kirkham. Can't say that I blame you. He is rather pleasing to the eye. I caught a glimpse of his body in Macon when I walked into the wrong bathroom. On purpose, of course. He still didn't succumb to my powers, though, even when I dropped my own towel in shock." I counted to ten inside my head as I focused on breathing deeply. I would *not* react. She was testing me. I couldn't let her see that I had feelings for Oliver.

"I think you'll find that Oliver has better taste in women than you," I spat back sarcastically.

"You're really going there? I'm more of a woman than you'll ever be. I bet that blonde color is really from a bottle."

"Oh, because you're not fake at all," I snorted. "Are your tits even real? They get bigger each year."

"I'm not staying here to be insulted. If you have any questions about the contacts, you can call Miles. He has all the information, too."

"I wasn't planning on asking you anyway," I called as she stormed toward my door.

"You have one huge fucking chip on your shoulder, Jade!" she yelled. "This isn't over!"

"Whatever," I yawned, not even looking at her. When I heard my door slam, I chuckled to myself.

I had to admit I didn't like the idea of Oliver going to Russia with Alicia for two weeks. I'd have to do something drastic to make sure he didn't forget me while he was over there with her.

✽ ✽ ✽

"I like your use of color, Jade," Brian mused, looking over my designs. I continued to edge around the table. Even though I was with four other designers, the creep kept standing next to *me*. "I could use this design in any of my showcase apartments all over the world." He wasn't impressing me with his wealth. In fact, I couldn't wait to leave this damn job. I just needed a good excuse first.

"Oh, I don't know about that. These colors would be too bright for Europe," one of the designers countered. She'd been giving me the bitch brow all morning. "I'd take out the orange, too."

"I disagree," the tanned man, whose name I kept forgetting, replied. "You need the warmth. It's a gallery, remember. I think it works."

"The design itself is a piece of art," Brian grinned, nudging me with his shoulder. "Well done, Jade." Wow! All this praise and I was only *pretending* to be an interior designer. "Okay, I think it's time to break for lunch."

I looked down at my phone to check the time, noticing I had a message from Oliver.

What time are you taking lunch today? I'm not sure I can wait until tomorrow night to see you.

My heart inflated when I read his words. A lunch date, too. I really was starting to crack his defenses.

I typed a quick response while the others in the room were chatting with each other.

Actually, I'm having lunch right now. Where did you want to meet? Shall I come to your office? J xx

His reply was instant.

No, I'll meet you outside my building. In…10 minutes. Is that okay with you?

That's fine. See you soon. :) x

I figured his response was because he didn't want any of his employees to see us together. I tried to rise above it, but it still hurt a little.

"Jade, did you want to join me for lunch?" Brian called as I looked up from my phone.

"Oh, I'm sorry. I have plans to meet someone."

"Oliver?" he glared, raising an eyebrow.

"Yes," I smiled, picking my bag up. "I'll see you in an hour."

* * *

Oliver was already waiting for me outside his building. How a guy could look so delectable just standing there in a dark suit was beyond me, but I had the familiar ache in between my legs as I approached him.

"Hey," I called from behind him. Once again, he struck me down with those deadly dark eyes of his as he turned around to face me.

"Hi," he sighed, taking a deep breath in. He looked really stressed.

"Are you okay?" I asked, touching his shoulder.

"It's been a long morning. I just needed to get out of the

office for an hour."

"Trouble running your empire?" I smirked.

"Something like that." He ran his hands through his hair, watching me. "So where are we having lunch?"

"You asked me on this lunch date. Shouldn't you already have an idea?"

Oliver's face softened before he spoke. "Lunch date? That's what you think this is?"

"Yes, and don't even try to deny it," I countered, putting my hands on my hips. I'd worn a dark blue suit today in an attempt to stop Brian's delusional advances toward me, but Oliver still gazed over my body, almost trying to unwrap me with his eyes.

"How long do you have for lunch?" he asked, clearing his throat as he showed me to his car. It was a black Audi.

"An hour. Where's the limo?" I gasped.

"I do drive myself places, Jade," he chuckled, opening the door for me.

"This is a nice car," I purred, stroking the leather seats. "What model is it?"

"An Audi R8 Knight," he muttered, starting the engine.

"Was it named after Knight Rider with David Hasselhoff?"

"No, Jade," he snorted, shaking his head as he pulled out into traffic.

"What music are you listening to at the moment?" I questioned, reaching forward to check his playlist on the built-in stereo. The Killers came up first. "The Killers, huh?"

"They're a talented band." I nodded in agreement, pressing random play.

"Is this playlist about me?" I asked as *Bad Romance* by Lady

Gaga began to play. How varied was Oliver's taste?

"Mostly, yes. I kept finding songs that reminded me of you and the playlist grew."

"Mm…what else is on here? You should have songs like Toxic and Tainted Love."

"You think I've hated you these last six months?"

"I would," I admitted, looking out the window.

"I don't hate you, Jade. I may have been disappointed, but I could never hate you."

"So, you created a Jade playlist instead. Oliver, that's the kind of thing a teenage boy would do. You're not thinking about giving me a mixed tape, are you?" I teased, trying to lighten the conversation.

"God, I've missed this," he laughed, darting his eyes toward me.

"My random conversations?" I asked with a giggle.

"That, and having an escape from work."

"Has it been *that* stressful today?"

"You wouldn't believe me if I told you about the level of stress I have on my shoulders right now."

"You can always talk to me, you know. Okay, I might not understand a word you're saying, but if it helps relieve the stress, I'll gladly pretend to be interested."

"I wouldn't even know where to start. Plus, some of the information I deal with could put you in danger. My line of work isn't easy, Jade. Sometimes I feel as if I'm helping the devil himself." His voice sounded strained, and I knew I should have pushed him for more information. My mission depended on it. In this instance, however, my heart was overruling my head. I was worried for the man I loved. The mission could wait.

"I want you to trust me again, Oliver. If that means helping you with your burdens, I'll do it. I need you to understand what you mean to me."

"You're so confusing. One minute you're telling me I let my feelings overrule everything and that's what pushed you away. Now you're telling me you want me to understand what I mean to you. You can't keep giving me these mixed signals. How am I supposed to figure out where to go from here? I need to know—what do I *mean* to you, Jade?"

It was easier talking to him when he had to keep his eyes on the road. I wasn't distracted by his reactions.

"I came back. Doesn't that answer your question?"

"Always so cryptic," he muttered more to himself than anything. "If this is meant to be helping my stress, it isn't."

"You mean *a lot* to me," I whispered close to his ear. The car swerved a little, and I had to wonder if my closeness was affecting him.

"I've always known that," he exhaled, pulling into a parking lot.

"You're taking me to lunch at Wendy's?" I giggled as he pulled around to the drive thru.

"You only have an hour for lunch and I wanted to talk to you, too. Where did you think I'd take you?"

"I'm not sure."

"I try not to let money define me, remember?" I did remember. That was one of the many things I loved about him.

"You really love fast food, don't you?"

"Mrs. Davis hardly lets me eat it. It's a nice treat for me," he admitted sheepishly. "Plus, it is a quick lunch. We can eat in the car."

"What a date," I teased.

"What do you want, a burger, chicken, maybe a salad?"

"If you're having a burger so will I. I can't watch you eat one if I only have a salad."

"Okay, two burgers it is, then. Coke? Is that okay, too?" I nodded in agreement.

"What's so funny?" Oliver asked once we'd pulled over to eat our food.

"How much did this car cost roughly?"

"Around one hundred and twenty thousand dollars. Why?"

"We're eating fast food in it, that's why. You've even let me set my fries on your dashboard."

"It's just a car, Jade. I have plenty of others." He was so casual as he spoke. He didn't let the money take over his life, but I did wonder how he would cope without it. Being rich was all he had ever known.

"Sorry, Mr. Rich," I quipped. "I forgot you must have about twenty cars."

"Only seven, actually," he quipped, taking a deep pull on the straw in his soda. "Not counting the limo."

"Why would you need *seven* cars?"

"Most stay with my different properties." I guess that made sense. "How's your car? Do you still have that blue mercedes?"

"Yes, but it's in storage back home. There was no point taking it with me. I was…um…traveling around a lot," I winced, taking a handful of fries.

"I'm aware of that, Jade," he sighed, dabbing his mouth with a paper napkin. Damn, he ate that quickly. I still had half of my fries to eat.

"Oh yes, you had my bank account tracked. Do you do that a lot?" I mumbled through a mouthful of food.

"You were the first. Look, I'm sorry. I only wanted to know you were safe. If I had tracked you down...I might not have followed through with my plan to go to you."

"Really?" I widened my eyes. I didn't believe him because of the lengths he went to find me. No target had ever gotten as close to discovering a lead before. Miles had to work double time to knock Oliver off my scent.

"Okay, probably not. I still would have gone to you," he admitted, defeated. "I'm sorry about tracking your account. Truly, I am."

"Did you search for anything else?" I had fake accounts for Jade Gibbs, but my family's first names and history were the same. My past wasn't something I was ready to talk about, even if it was fake. How much did Oliver know about me? Miles had said Oliver hadn't delved in too deeply yet, but I needed to be sure.

"What do you mean?" he frowned, searching my face.

"What else did you find out about me?" I snapped, reaching for my drink. My mouth was suddenly really dry.

"Nothing, Jade, I swear. I wouldn't invade your private life like that. If there was something, I'd want to hear it from you. The tracker was all about your safety, you have to believe me. I was worried you might have been kidnapped. It may sound ridiculous, but you don't know the pressure I'm under. So many people want the information I have. You would have been an easy target." *Oh Oliver, you have no idea.* There was more chance of him being kidnapped than me. Not that I would *ever* let that happen.

"Okay," I sighed, eating my last few fries. "I understand, but don't *ever* do anything like that again."

"As long as I know you're safe, I won't need to," he muttered, running his hand through my hair gently. "I've missed this," he breathed, looking down at my mouth. I couldn't help darting my tongue out, moistening my lips in case he kissed me. "I'm so conflicted right now." He pulled away, slumping back into his seat.

"What's wrong?"

"My mind is telling me one thing while my body is saying another."

"This isn't going to be an easy fix. I understand that. We just need time. Don't over analyze everything."

"You know that isn't easy for me."

"It's only been a few days. This is strange for me, too."

"In what way?" he pleaded. "Do you wish you hadn't come back?"

"No," I sighed, shaking my head. "Most of me wishes I'd never left in the first place. That I could have been stronger."

"I wish you hadn't gone, too," he admitted, leaning in closer. "Who knows where we could have been by now."

"We still have time."

"I know we do," he smirked, looking down at his phone when it began to ring. "Yes," he answered curtly. "I'm out having lunch. Why?" I sat there watching him, my eyes tracing over every line and contour of him. I loved everything about his face as he listened to whomever was speaking to him on the phone, from the slight stubble on his chin, to the worry lines on his forehead as he frowned. "I don't care if she has to wait. You can tell Imogen that if she has an issue, she can take it up with me later. She shouldn't even be trying to muscle in on this meeting. It's none of her damn business!" I had to hold my legs together as I watched him get all assertive. He was sex on legs. Add in the fact I was madly in love with him, and I had one hell of a mission this time. "I'm heading back now, Alicia." Oliver looked up, grinning at me. He must have noticed my disapproving face at learning it was Alicia on the other end of the phone. "I took my car, not that it's any of your business. I'll be back in ten minutes. You can tell Imogen if she insists on crashing my meeting, she can wait!" With that, he hung up.

"Problems in the office?" I asked, genuinely concerned.

"You could say that," he stressed, pulling at his hair before gripping the steering wheel. "I need to cut our lunch date short. I'm sorry, Jade."

"Don't worry about it. It's not like you're canceling our dinner date tomorrow." I grabbed my trash and put everything in the bag. "Let me throw this away first. I don't want your car to smell like fast food for days." I could feel his eyes on me as I stepped out of his car and walked over to put the empty wrappers and leftover soda in the trash can.

"What time did you want me to pick you up tomorrow?" he asked once I was sitting beside him again.

"Any time after seven works for me." We made small talk on the way back, finalizing our plans for the following evening. By the time we pulled up outside his building, we had decided on him picking me up at eight outside my hotel.

"Thanks for meeting me for lunch, Jade," he muttered with his hands in his pockets. Could he feel the electricity charging between us, too? Was that why his hands were in his pockets? Was he trying to restrain himself?

"You're welcome. I'm sorry I couldn't be more help. I hope the rest of your day goes okay."

"You helped, Jade." He spoke softly, studying my lips again. It was pure torture having to hold back. "I'll see you tomorrow night."

"Okay," I replied, watching him as he started to walk off. Just before he reached the automatic doors, I called out to him. "Thanks for lunch."

"It was my pleasure," he responded with a dreamy smirk. "I look forward to seeing you tomorrow." Then he was gone. That was Oliver Kirkham, the charmer.

* * *

I spent the night looking through the contacts that Alicia had thrown at me a few days ago. It wouldn't do any harm to get ahead on this mission and figure out which associates I could rule out. As I went through everything, I realized that Alicia had been pretty thorough; I had to give her some credit. She was good at one thing—research.

By the time I'd gone through the list, I counted at least thirty names I'd have to investigate. This mission was almost impossible, but if anyone could do it, I could.

I was checking through my emails when a knock came at my door. It was pretty late, so I wasn't sure who would be coming to see me at this time of the night. Deep down, I knew the one face I wanted to see behind the door.

As I opened my door to find Alicia standing on the other side, I sighed deeply. What was her problem?

"What the hell do you want at this time?" I glared as she pushed past me, entering my bedroom.

"Sonia wants a progress report from both of us. Have you checked your emails?"

"Not in the last hour. I've been doing some research on the associates on that list you gave me."

"Did you find anything?"

"No. I think you've covered all the possible candidates."

"Hopefully the trip to Russia will give me a few new leads. Oliver is meeting with several scientists. If only I knew what some of his code names were."

"Don't think for a second that you have this mission, Alicia. Oliver and I have a bond that can't be broken. He's weakening each time we see each other."

"Two weeks is a long time," she gloated, flicking her hair behind her shoulders.

"You came here tonight just to gloat about being alone with him for two weeks, didn't you?"

"Yep," she sneered. "And to do this progress report. Although, I have more to tell Sonia than you." I could have risen to her comment, but I was too tired. I just wanted to get the damn report done so she would leave.

"I'll see you when I'm back from Russia," Alicia called over her shoulder as she was leaving a while later. "Don't worry, I'll take *good* care of Oliver." I closed my door without a response. She was such a bitch. She seemed to forget one thing, though. I still had my dinner date with Oliver before Russia.

CHAPTER SIX

"You look beautiful, Jade," Oliver grinned, opening his car door for me. I'd opted for a beautiful red dress with lace trim tonight. It was elegant and sexy at the same time. I also knew he loved me in red.

"No limo again?" I teased.

"What can I say, I like driving you around."

"Where have you decided to take me for dinner, then?"

"I thought we could do Italian again, if that's okay. I know a small little restaurant that has the best pasta in town."

"That sounds good to me."

"How was your day?" he asked, pulling out into traffic. "Has Brian made any more advances?"

"I told you I can handle him," I chuckled. "I didn't see him much today, though. He's heading out of town for a few days."

"Good," Oliver muttered under his breath. "I meant what I said about him. Please be careful." I nodded, turning to gaze out the window. "I may sound like a broken record, but I care about you, Jade. That's *never* changed."

"You don't know how happy that makes me to hear that," I sighed, turning so our eyes could meet.

"Do you still care about me?"

"What do you think?" I whispered, studying his face. "I know it's hard for you to understand why I left without any warning, but I didn't run for the reason you're thinking."

"I put too much pressure on you. I get it now, but you could have talked to me about it, Jade. Running like that…"

I was conflicted. Did I just lay my heart on the line and tell him how I really felt? If I wanted him to be thinking of me the entire time he was in Russia it was the only option, but was I ready to be that open with him? Luckily, we pulled up outside the restaurant before I had to answer.

"Wow, this place is great," I gasped, taking in the small candlelit table for two. It was so secluded, too.

"Yeah, I figured this would be a good place for us to talk. It doesn't get too noisy here, and you don't feel as if other tables can overhear your conversation." Oliver pulled a chair out for me before taking his own seat.

"Do you come here a lot?" I questioned.

"Are you asking if I bring other women here? Didn't you ask me the same thing in London the weekend we met?"

"I was going to ask your opinion on the menu, actually," I sniggered.

Oliver laughed with me before suddenly becoming serious, taking my hands in his over the table. "What do you want from me, Jade? I've tried to be strong, but when it comes to you, I can't. I need to know what you want and that you'll talk to me. No more running."

"I'm not going anywhere, I promise." It was only a partial lie. If Oliver and I were ever going to get our happily ever after, we would have to have some time apart. There was no reason to think about that right now, though.

"I want to believe you, Jade. I really do."

"We don't have to have all the answers right now. Why

can't we just see how it goes?"

"I thought that was what we were doing?" he smirked.

"Okay, smart ass," I giggled. "Can we stop with the heavy, then? Why don't you tell me about your day? You seemed really stressed yesterday at lunch."

"You noticed that, huh?"

"I know you pretty well." I looked at our hands that were still linked together.

"My uncle and I are disagreeing over an important development in the company. He thinks his age should give him the upper hand, but he isn't thinking rationally."

"But it's your company. You don't have to listen to him, do you?" I was trying to act dumb. I knew Richard owned a percentage of Kirkham Industries, but that Oliver held the majority.

"It may be my company, but my uncle does have a small claim on it. Not enough to allow him to overrule me, though. I value his opinion most of the time. This time, however, I feel like he's being driven by money."

"Is that what it's about? Money?"

"No," Oliver sighed. "Money is the least of my problems. I have a lot of power in my hands, Jade. There are times I feel as if I'm playing God. One choice could affect the entire world."

"That sounds tough."

"It is," he sighed, glancing behind me. Our food had arrived.

"You weren't kidding about this place having the best pasta. It's really good," I mumbled, digging into my meal.

"Yeah, I'm rarely wrong," he winked with a smile.

"So, these important decisions you have to make…are

they always top secret?"

"Mostly, yes."

"I'm starting to understand why you've met so many world leaders."

"I'm not going to tire you with the boring details of my job, Jade."

"I don't mind, really."

"You're really okay with me talking about fusion and power cores?" My heart began to race. Power cores? Would it really be that easy? I was about to find out.

"Power cores?" I frowned, sipping my drink.

"You really want me to go into detail?" he chuckled.

"Not too much. I need to be able to understand what you're saying," I giggled.

"Okay, well, with nuclear weapons they have to have a core. This consists of heat and energy. There are two types of nuclear weapons—those that use most of their energy from fission alone, and those that simply use fission to begin the reaction."

"You really are a nerd, aren't you?" I smirked.

"You knew that about me the day we met," he chuckled. "We don't have to talk about work."

"What did you want to talk about?"

"You," he grinned with a gleam in his eye. "Why don't you tell me where you've been these last six months?"

"You tracked my account. You probably know better than me where I've been."

He chuckled. "I guess I deserved that."

"I traveled around a lot. Mostly I stayed with friends. I had some money put away, so I just kept running."

"What made you finally stop?" His eyes were intense as he waited for me to answer.

"I woke up to my true feelings." I reached my hand over toward his. "I wasn't running from you. I was running from my feelings *for* you," I admitted. "It was all happening so fast and it scared me. I've never been dependent on someone before. I've only ever had to look out for myself. Relationships aren't easy for me, Oliver. They never have been."

"You should have told me." He traced the top of my hand with his fingertips. "All these months that have been wasted. I've been going out of my mind trying to find you, Jade."

"I'm sorry. I never meant to hurt you."

"I know," he sighed. "I'm starting to see that now."

After our dinner, we shared a dessert again. He said he wasn't that hungry, but I figured it had more to do with being able to feed me the delicious ice cream from his own spoon than anything else.

"You've been watching my mouth the entire night," I giggled as he fed me the last spoonful of ice cream.

"I have?" he teased, licking his lips. "You do have mesmerizing lips."

"They can't be that good. You haven't even tried to kiss me properly since I've been back," I challenged, raising my eyebrows.

"All in good time," he breathed, looking down at his watch. "Did you want anything else? Coffee? More ice cream?"

"I'm good, thanks."

"I have some bad news before we go any further tonight." I knew what was coming and braced myself. I'd been wondering when he would bring up his trip to Russia. "I'm leaving for

Russia this weekend. I'll be gone for two weeks."

"What?" I gasped. "You're going away for *two weeks* and you only decided to tell me this now?"

"It was never the right time. I can't get out of it, Jade. It's a really important trip."

"Two weeks is such a long time," I moped, fiddling with the tablecloth.

"If I could take you with me, I would, but my uncle will be there. It would just get too complicated and I need to focus."

"Oh, let me guess, your PA is going," I glared, crossing my arms.

"You really don't like Alicia, do you?"

"No," I glared. "You don't trust Brian, and I don't trust her!"

"Now you're being ridiculous."

"I don't think I am. So, are you cutting our dinner date short so you can get ready for Russia with your hot PA?"

"Is she hot? I hadn't really noticed."

"You can be such a jerk sometimes," I glared, standing up quickly. I was becoming angry to elicit a reaction from him. I needed to know I was the one he wanted, not Alicia.

"Where are you going?"

"You can take me back to my hotel now. I wouldn't want to make you late for your flight!"

"It's not until tomorrow afternoon," he said, following me outside. "Jade, slow down."

"Do you know what I don't get?" I snapped as I turned around to face him. "Why tell me you wanted to give us another try if you were going to Russia for two weeks?"

"I didn't want to wait. I needed to know where we stood before I went."

"I think it has more to do with you wanting to keep your distance from me," I countered.

"You really think that?" he asked, taking a step toward me.

"I know I'm right. Oliver, you've barely touched me since I came back. You've never had this kind of control around me before."

"Jade, I'm keeping my distance because the moment I let go, I'll be lost in you again." His eyes grew darker as he pushed me against the side of his car.

"Just let go," I whispered. "What's the worst that could happen?"

"You could break my heart again," he whispered, running his hands into my hair. "A man like me can't be left vulnerable. I have to think about my business, too."

"I won't do that again. You must see what you mean to me…how much I care."

"I thought you didn't want to be controlled by your feelings?" he muttered, stroking my face with the back of his hand.

"I lied. It's my *feelings* that scare the crap out of me, because being away from you all that time only made them stronger. I can't run from how I feel anymore. I *need* to be with you!" I swallowed hard, watching his lips move toward mine as he took in what I was saying. *Yes, Oliver, I love you!*

As his lips pressed softly against mine, I sighed and wrapped my arms around his neck, drawing him closer to me.

I was sure he was going to pull away, but to my surprise, he pushed me against his car, crashing his body and mouth harder against mine.

His kiss was all consuming. I could feel his hand in my

hair gently tugging it. I groaned when our tongues collided passionately, having forgotten how good he tasted. Every sweep of my tongue was met with his in a timeless dance. Sparks seemed to be igniting all over my body. Oliver was bringing me back to life with his tender kiss.

"Mmm, I've missed those lips," he purred, pulling back when the kiss finally came to an end. "As much as I want to ask you to come back to my place, I think we should wait until I get back from Russia."

"Are you trying to say I'm the kind of girl who would sleep with a guy on their first date?" I teased. My arms were still wrapped around his neck and I loved the closeness.

"I know you are," he chuckled, leaning down to peck my lips once more.

"Only when it comes to you. But you're right. We should wait. We're taking this slowly, remember?"

"I know," he sighed, pulling me into him for another deep kiss. This time his hands began to slide down the side of my body. *Oliver going slowly?* Was that even possible?

I giggled against his mouth when his hands finally grabbed my ass. "This is slowly for you?"

"Yep," he grinned, finally pulling back. "Come on. Let's get you back to your hotel before I lose complete control."

"Good idea," I sniggered, letting him open the car door for me.

"It's funny how quickly things can go back to normal, huh?" He started his engine. "I really wish I could cut this trip short."

"What's the trip about?"

"It's mostly meetings with N.A.T.O, but I have a few

associates I'm scheduled to meet with, too."

"No world leaders this time?"

"There will be some," he muttered, unaffected by that statement. I was a Seductor and meeting certain world leaders would unnerve *me*. It wasn't uncommon for them to be assigned as targets, so I had met a few. Oliver, though, was sitting there unfazed at the fact that he would be conversing with them while he was in Russia.

"Does nothing faze you?"

"What do you mean?" he asked, glancing at me quickly.

"Nothing scares you, does it?"

"In my job, no, but other things in my life do."

"Like what?"

"Losing my father one day," he sighed, staring at the traffic ahead of us. "I know he's almost gone already, but the thought of never seeing him again terrifies me." My heart ached for him. It was clear how much he idolized his father. "Then there's you."

"*Me?*" I questioned.

"I can't think rationally when I'm around you, Jade. That's a dangerous position for a man like me to be in."

"Don't you realize that I feel the same way when I'm around you? Oliver, you have no idea what I've been through these last six months. I tried to forget you, but I couldn't get you out of my head!"

"Doesn't that tell you something?" he grinned, pulling up outside my hotel. Why did it have to be so close to the restaurant? I looked at him quizzically. "You need to listen to your body. You can't deny what it wants. I've been trying to tell you that since the moment we met."

"I know," I sighed, leaning in to peck his lips. "My body

wants only you. I've always known that." My statement stirred a low growl from within his chest, and before I could blink, his lips were pressed hard against mine.

"Fuck," he moaned, fumbling with his seat belt. "You better get inside. I only have so much restraint."

"Will you call me once you've landed in Russia?" I pouted, not wanting to move an inch as his lips began to move down my neck.

"Of course I will. When I get back, I promise we can try again. I won't bring up the last six months. We'll just start fresh and see where things go. I'll go as slow as you need, Jade. I want you to open up to me." I smiled against his lips, drowning in his words. This didn't feel like a mission. I'd been given a second chance to fall deeper in love with him, and I didn't want to waste a moment of it.

"I want that, too. You have no idea." I moaned against his mouth as he captured my lips once more.

"Now get out of here before I hold you hostage and take you to Russia with me," he chuckled, breaking our heated kiss.

"Where did all this control come from? Do you really want to wait until you get back from Russia? You know how good we are together," I purred, tugging on his tie. My body was aching for him.

"Jade, if we do anything tonight, I won't last two weeks without you."

"So, you haven't…in the last six months…" I trailed off.

"No, I haven't been with anyone since you." He smiled warmly, running his hand through my hair. "So you can imagine all the things I want to do to you." I held my thighs together, watching his hooded gaze on my legs. "One night wouldn't be enough time for me, Jade. I'd need *days* to be even partially satisfied." I swallowed hard, closing my eyes as he trailed his fingertips across the top of my breasts. "When I get back, I'll make it up to you. I promise." He pressed his lips softly to mine quickly. "Now go before I change my mind."

"Okay," I pouted, opening my eyes and finally getting out the car. "Make sure you call me."

"I will," he chuckled, rolling his window down. "I'll see you soon, Beautiful." My heart inflated when I heard his nickname for me.

Oliver really was beginning to forgive me. The only problem now was figuring out how I would cope without him for two weeks.

CHAPTER SEVEN

"It's all under control, Sonia. Oliver wants to try again when he gets back from Russia." I stretched, opening the documents she'd just sent me.

"I knew it wouldn't take you long. Hopefully Alicia will get some information you can use when she returns. At least this assignment with Zara will keep you busy this week. She's becoming quite a force to be reckoned with."

I skimmed over the documents. "We're working with the FBI?" I gasped, looking at the client's name.

"Off the records, yes. They've been trying to bring down our target for years. He has a soft spot for blondes." That would explain Zara and me taking this case. "They just need a location. The moment you find him, they'll take over." I knew from past experience it was never that easy when we worked with the FBI.

"There's a lot of violence in these notes, Sonia. What are you getting Zara and me into?" I questioned. The more I read, the clearer it became that this was a very dangerous mission. Our target wasn't only a murderer, but a rapist, too. I wasn't concerned for myself because I'd undertaken missions like it before, but Zara was still inexperienced.

"I know you girls can handle it, but I want two of you on the case just to be safe. The fact that you're already in New York is perfect!"

"When is Zara flying out?"

"Tomorrow. That will give you time to go over the documents and decide the best plan of action. Mr. Monroe mixes with some very dangerous company, so you'll need to tread carefully and make sure you have a good escape plan mapped out. Don't let yourselves be trapped before you can make the call."

"Okay. I'll do some research tonight."

"Zara will be bringing all your new gadgets with her. Miles insisted on you having the newest available models."

"Okay."

"You're focused on this mission with Mr. Kirkham, aren't you? You can't let your feelings control you, Jade. Not yet. I need your head clear for this side job, too."

"It's all under control. You still haven't sent my agreement about my identity when I leave the Seductors, though," I reminded her.

"I'm working on it."

"Which means it hasn't been authorized yet!" I snapped. "Sonia, you promised me!"

"Acquire this steal and our founder will give you anything you want. The contract is being drawn up as we speak. Relax, Jade!"

"What if this power core doesn't even exist? Will I still be able to go to him?" How could I even trust them?

"We'll cross that bridge when we reach it."

"When we *reach* it?" I yelled, completely losing it. "I accepted this mission because you offered me the Jade *Gibbs* identity when I completed my contract! I'm not walking away from Oliver for good. Whether he waits for me or not, I'm still going to him the moment my contract is over. I don't care what you do!"

"What happened to you, Jade?" Sonia sighed. "You had so much promise."

"I'm still the same Seductor, Sonia. I just have something to live for now when I leave."

"I never thought you'd fall for a target." The disappointment in her voice was clear.

"Yet you assign me to him again. You can't be *that* angry with me."

"I have to admit, for once it will work in our favor. Even if it does go against Seductor rules."

"How did I get away with breaking a rule?"

"You were just lucky. This mission is unlike anything we've ever dealt with before, Jade. Most rules aren't applicable with this one. You must know what you're involved in."

"I do," I muttered.

"Good. Zara will call you when she arrives. She might as well stay with you. When are you moving into your apartment?"

"In a few days." At least Zara could help me settle in, not that much would need to be done. The apartment was fully furnished.

"Well, she can stay with you there, too. If Mr. Kirkham returns, you can say she's an old friend of yours. I'll expect a progress report from the two of you in a few days." With that, she hung up.

I didn't like the idea of still being on the mission when Oliver returned.

Staying up late that night, I researched and finished reading all the documents on Mr. Monroe. I wanted to get this assignment over with as quickly as possible.

* * *

"Oh. My. God! What a trip," Zara moaned, walking into my hotel room the next evening. "I've already checked in. I'm on the floor below yours. Sonia said she sent all the paperwork over yesterday. So, what's the plan?"

"Hi, Zara. It's nice to see you, too," I chuckled.

"Sorry. I've been stressing over this mission all week. Have you seen this target's background?"

"Yes," I exhaled. "We'll need to watch each other's backs. I've done a sweep of the club already. Mr. Monroe has definitely been there."

"And?"

"He was there two days ago. I checked the CCTV."

"How did you manage that?"

"The security guard let me take a look," I winked. "I've mapped out the black areas in the club, too. We need to make sure we aren't left alone in any of these spots," I stated, pulling up blueprints of the nightclub and then pointing out the dark areas. "Mr. Monroe has his own private room in the back here, with his own servers and dancers so no one can tip off the cops. It's close to an escape route so he can slip away if anyone comes for him." Zara was studying the plans as I spoke. "You need to be wary of these men. They are ruthless and will take what they want, no questions asked." She swallowed hard. "Do you understand what I mean?"

"Yes," she murmured. "You won't leave me alone, will you, Jade?"

"Not if I can help it. Sonia already said we need to stick together. This mission is too dangerous to do alone." All she did was nod. "These missions will get easier, Zara."

"I know. It's just that I get used to doing one type of mission, then I get moved to something else. I've never had to defend myself before."

"It might not even come to that. As soon as we confirm that Mr. Monroe is in the club, we only have to make sure he stays there until the FBI storms the building."

"You make it sound so easy."

"It will be," I beamed, trying to reassure her. "Why don't you get some rest? We can go over the plan in the morning."

"Okay," she smiled, moving in for a hug. "It's good to see you, Jade. It's been months."

"I know," I chuckled, hugging her back. "Now, get some rest. It's going to be a long few days."

* * *

Mr. Monroe was a difficult man to track down. He didn't visit the club for the first three nights after Zara arrived, but that gave us time to stake out the nightclub. Not to mention, I finally moved into my small apartment. When he finally was spotted again, Zara was more relaxed about the mission.

"Is that his right hand man?" she whispered into my ear while we both scanned the crowd in the club.

"Yes, I think it might be," I replied, stretching for a better look. Mr. Monroe's right hand man was with three other men that I recognized from the files Sonia sent over. "You see the guy in the grey suit next to him?" Zara nodded. "That's the guy we need to be wary of. Do *not* allow yourself to be alone with him."

"Got it."

"Do you have your taser?" She held up her bag. "Is it on full power? These bastards deserve it."

"Yes," she giggled.

"What about your hair pins?" Miles was a genius. He'd invented hair pins with a paralyzer substance inside them that we could inject into an attacker. They would be paralyzed for over half an hour. Zara tilted her head, showing me the pins.

"Okay, then we're good to go."

Together, we walked into the center of the club. I could feel eyes on us as we crossed the dance floor toward the bar. We were both dressed to draw attention, and it didn't take long before we were hit on.

"Are your feet tired?" a guy slurred at me, leaning against the bar. I'd heard this pick up line so many times before and internally rolled my eyes. "Because you've been running through my mind all day, Sexy."

"How original," I sighed. "Have you *ever* picked up a woman with that line?"

The guy frowned, thinking hard before answering. "Actually, no, I haven't."

"Then it's time to change your tactics," I snorted, turning away from him. The dangerous guy in the grey suite was closer to us now. He was already checking Zara out from behind. I couldn't wait to take the asshole right in the crotch!

"What do you want to drink?" I asked Zara.

"Allow me to get these ladies," a male voice called from behind me. Zara widened her eyes, so I knew it was Mr. Dangerous. "What are you having?"

"No, really, we can get our own drinks," I glared, turning to face him. Jeez, he was tall and well built.

"I won't take no for an answer," he smirked, pushing me up against the bar. I couldn't move. The asshole! "What are you and your friend having, Sexy?"

"If you're going to insist, we'll have a vodka and coke please." I looked over at Zara. She had a worried look on her face. Yes, the guy was huge, but I knew we could handle it.

"I haven't seen you two here before," he mused, looking out into the crowd before handing us our drinks.

"We're from out of town. Well, my friend is. I only moved to New York a few weeks ago," I muttered, glancing down at the floor.

"Do you ladies want to go somewhere more private and exclusive?"

"You mean leave the club?" Zara frowned. "We've only just arrived."

"No, the club has a private room out the back. It's only reserved for sexy ladies like you."

"A private room, you say?" I smiled. "Well, lead the way." I winked at Zara as we followed him out through the back. We needed to make sure Mr. Monroe wasn't going anywhere before we could trigger the alarm, letting the FBI know he was there. We'd need to stun or paralyze him before we left, though. That meant we would have to take out all of his men, too, or try to get Mr. Monroe alone somehow.

My eyes widened as we entered the back room. There had to be at least ten men standing around or sitting, drinking and laughing. Some had strippers on their laps and were happily 'getting it on.'

"I'm not sure this is our kind of party." I pretended to act flustered, taking in all the greedy eyes looking at Zara and me.

"Oh, I don't think you have the choice to leave now," a stocky man sneered, coming up behind me. "We want you to stay."

"I...I have a boyfriend," I stuttered, trying to work out the best plan of action. I couldn't see Zara and me being able to stick together. We'd need to split up if we stood any chance of getting close to Mr. Monroe. Quickly scanning the crowd, I realized he wasn't there. I did, however, notice a few doors in the far corner of the room.

"Do you think that would stop me?" the guy chuckled darkly, pulling me hard against his chest. "Come on, you know you want me." I began to fight against him, hitting his chest as he started to drag me toward a side door. I was gripping my purse tightly, and as soon as we were out of view, I was going to make this guy pay. If there was one type of man that I hated more than anything, it was one who took a woman without asking, or thinking about the consequences or the damage they were inflicting when they did. They were monsters and deserved to pay in an extremely agonizing way. My eyes darted toward Zara before I was pulled out of sight. Mr. Dangerous was making advances toward her, and I really hoped she could handle it. She'd trained for missions like this, so I knew she had the skills.

"I'm going to fuck you so hard," my attacker growled, pulling me into a room. The moment the door closed; I switched character. This asshole was going *down*.

"Actually, asshole, you're not," I glared, squaring my shoulders and awaiting his attack.

"Oh, you want to play it this way?" He laughed darkly,

licking his lips. "It turns me on when a girl resists so much. I hope you're a screamer, too." The rage in me was burning into pure fury!

The asshole made his move, trying to grab my wrists. I flicked my hands up, spun around, and pressed my purse against his neck, tazing him on full power. His body began to jerk and convulse from the intense shock.

"Men like you make me sick! I hope you rot in hell when your time comes," I spat just before he fell to the ground.

After ten minutes, I ripped my dress and ruffled my hair into a mess, then stunned the asshole again. I didn't want him waking up anytime soon. Zara had already messaged me to say she'd taken out the other asshole. He'd dragged her into a coat closet, so she'd left him there. She'd already gone back out to try and find Mr. Monroe.

I opened the door, stumbling out. No one was watching me, but I noticed Zara was straddling a guy. As she moved, I smirked. She'd found Mr. Monroe. Now all we had to do was get him alone, which might not be too difficult.

"Zara," I stressed, "we need to go!" Mr. Monroe looked around her at me, his eyes widening as he took me in.

"You're leaving already? But we only just met."

"Yes, I don't feel safe here!" I spat.

"I have a back room. You'll feel safe there. Have one drink with me at least. Your friend can join us, too."

"I...I..."

"You'll be safer there than out here. I can't control my men around sexy woman like you."

"One drink," I replied, allowing Mr. Monroe to lead us into his back room.

The new space we entered was an office with a large leather couch. Mr. Monroe locked the door before turning to smile at both of us.

"Do you feel safer now?" he asked as Zara sat next to me on the couch, stroking my hair.

"A little," I muttered, looking around.

"You two are stunning," Mr. Monroe stated, pouring us a drink. "I'd pay good money to have you both in my bed tonight."

"Excuse me?" I choked. "Are you trying to infer that Zara and I are prostitutes?"

"Wait, Jade, hear him out. How much money are you talking about?" Zara asked with feigned interest. She was learning well.

"Name your price. I'll pay anything," he smirked.

"So, we'd go to your place and be alone? We don't want any of those men outside near us," I added. Getting Mr. Monroe alone at his hotel or wherever he was staying might work even better. He always used different aliases, so the FBI could never track him.

"You have my word. It would just be us."

"And what would we have to do?" Zara asked.

"Pleasure me, of course, and allow me to take you anyway I wish." Mr. Monroe licked his lips. "I'd also pay extra to watch you two pleasure each other." Yeah, like I didn't know that was coming.

"Two thousand dollars and you have a deal," Zara blurted out.

"Zara!" I hissed, playing my cover.

"What? Jade, that's a thousand each for *one* night. We need that money—you know we do." She turned to Mr Monroe. "Do we have a deal?"

"Yes, we do. Allow me to escort you ladies to my car."

❉ ❉ ❉

Mr. Monroe was staying in a hotel on the outskirts of town, which was perfect. I couldn't believe how well this mission had played out.

"When do we get our money?" Zara asked once we were inside his suite.

"Don't you trust me?" he chuckled, undoing his jacket. "Why don't the two of you strip? I want to see you. Then I'll pay up."

"Can I freshen up first?" I asked.

"Certainly." He gestured toward his bathroom.

I splashed my face before sending out the tracker code to the FBI, confirming Mr. Monroe's whereabouts. From what we had been told, Zara and I would have about ten minutes before they stormed the hotel.

When I walked back into the bedroom, Zara was already in her underwear, working her way down our target's body with her lips.

"Please join us, Jade," Mr. Monroe moaned as Zara bit down on his left nipple. I smirked, slipping out of my dress before stalking toward him. "Fuck, you two are stunning. I have no idea who to fuck first!" Zara sat up and straddled him, rocking herself against his erection. "Shit! Okay, Zara, you win. I'll take you first." He grabbed her breasts, pulling the cups of her bra down before sitting up to devour her naked skin. Zara looked over at me with a questioning look.

"What about me?" I pouted, removing the pins from my hair, allowing it to fall down my back. "Don't I get any attention?"

"Fuck! Girls, what are you *doing* to me?" he stressed, licking his lips before pulling me onto his lap instead. "Maybe I'll fuck you first. Shit, your tits are amazing!" He grabbed my breasts roughly, and the only thing that entered my mind was Oliver. No; I didn't want anyone else to touch me that way. Before I knew it, I'd ejected the pin into his neck, paralyzing him out of anger.

"Thank Christ that's over," Zara stressed, getting up and grabbing her clothes. "I take it you set off the tracker while you were in the bathroom?"

"Yes," I muttered, getting dressed, as well. Mr. Monroe was lying there with his eyes wide open. "I'm sorry, Mr. Monroe, but the FBI are on their way. They've been looking for you for a *long* time." His eyes showed pure rage, but of course he couldn't move. "Don't underestimate blondes in the future. They will be your undoing," I chuckled, winking at Zara.

"Goodbye, Mr. Monroe. It was *fun*," Zara giggled, grabbing her purse as we both turned around and walked out the door.

❊ ❊ ❊

"You did really well, Zara," I smiled, sipping my wine. We were back at our hotel having a drink in the bar.

"I thought I was going to lose it when I saw all those guys in the back room."

"You just have to keep a clear head, and you did. We work really well together."

"We really do," she beamed. I was about to speak when my phone rang. My heart skipped a beat at seeing Oliver's name flash across the screen.

"Excuse me," I muttered, taking my phone and walking out into the lobby. "Hey," I breathed, answering.

"Hi, Beautiful." I could hear the smile in his voice.

"How's it going? Have you gotten over the jetlag yet?"

"Almost," he chuckled. "How are you?"

"I'm fine. Maybe a little lonely," I admitted.

"Me, too. I can't wait until I can come home to you. I wish I'd brought you to Russia with me now." He could ignite so many feelings inside me with just a few words. He thought of me as home, which was something I'd never had before.

"It's funny how quickly things can go back to the way they were, huh?"

"Yes. I promise I'll go slow this time, though, Jade. We'll take this at the pace *you* want."

"I don't deserve you," I sighed. It was the truth. How could Oliver love me? It made no sense. Then again, he didn't know the real me. Would he still love me if he did?

"Why do you say that?"

"Ignore me. I'm just missing you, that's all. It's been so long since I've been with you. I'm starting to crave your touch."

"I know, Beautiful. I feel the same way. I'll be home soon, I promise, and when I am, I'm not going to let you leave my bed for weeks." I had to hold my legs together at his words and the timbre in his voice when he said them. I had to wait *two weeks*? That was too long!

"You're not helping my need for you, Oliver," I scolded.

"Sorry," he chuckled.

"You're not sorry," I teased.

"I wish you were here with me, Jade. I've got some really heavy meetings and social events to attend in the next few days. I could really use your calming influence," he sighed.

"You can call me any time—night or day. I'm here, Oliver."

"I know," he exhaled. "I've got to go for now, though. Alicia is calling me. I'll speak to you in a few days."

"Okay. Miss me."

"You know I will," he muttered before we both hung up.

"Was that 'the top target' calling?" Zara asked as I joined her back in the bar. I nodded. "Are you and Alicia really *both* on this mission?"

"Who told you that?"

"Jade, you know how it is at headquarters. The gossip is awful. So…who's winning? You or Alicia?"

"Well, Alicia has him all to herself for two weeks." I smiled sadly. "Does that answer your question? They're in Europe together."

"Then what are you still doing here? We've done our mission, book a damn flight. You can't let Alicia win this one. She'll never let you live it down if you do." Zara had a point. What the hell was I doing here? I *should* be in Russia!

"Can you email Sonia the progress report so our mission can be marked as complete?"

"Yes," she chuckled. "Now, *go!*"

CHAPTER EIGHT

The flight to Russia was long, but the anticipation of seeing Oliver kept me going. By the time I'd cleared my time off with Brian and booked my trip, it had been over a week since I'd seen him.

Russia had a bitter chill in the air. It didn't help that I'd arrived in the middle of the night, either. I wrapped my coat tighter around my body before catching a taxi to the hotel.

Oliver had called me almost every day since he'd left for his trip. I could only hope that me turning up like this was going to be a good surprise for him. He was worried about his uncle's reaction to me being back, which was why he hadn't asked me to go with him in the first place.

As I checked into the hotel, butterflies invaded my stomach at the knowledge that Oliver was in the same building somewhere. Probably curled up in bed, fast asleep. Images of bright white sheets caressing his body were driving me crazy.

When I got up to my room I took a shower, trying to calm the hunger that was seeping into my body. I needed to focus and not get carried away when I finally saw him. I had to make sure shy Jade was controlling the situation, not the *real* me. No matter how much I loved him, this was still a mission.

To get ready, I slipped into a tight red dress, knowing Oliver loved me in red. I completed the outfit with matching red underwear because it was the only way I could express the hellcat I really was. It saddened me to think about the future. Would he ever get the chance to know the real me? When I left the Seductors, I'd be coming back as Jade Gibbs. I'd have to act and lie my entire life. Could I really do that?

I finished straightening my hair and touched up my makeup before calling him. He was restless at night, so I half expected him to be awake.

He answered on the third ring. "Hello?"

"I didn't wake you, did I?" I stressed.

"No, Beautiful. I've been dozing on and off, but I haven't really slept yet," he soothed. "Are you okay? You don't usually call at this time?"

"I just needed to hear your voice."

"Missing me that much, huh?" he chuckled.

"You have no idea. I dreamt about you last night."

"Did you now? What kind of dream was it?"

"I think you know," I giggled.

"Christ, Jade, don't get me worked up. The night is when I crave you the most."

"Oliver, what would you do if I told you I was in the same hotel as you right now?" My body was trembling.

"Don't tease me, Jade," he pleaded.

"I'm not, Oliver," I whispered. "Tell me your room number and I'll prove it."

"Shit! Jade, if this is a joke it isn't funny. I'm in the Royal Suite on the top floor."

"Royal suite?" I giggled. "I think the money is finally getting to you."

"Stop teasing and get your sexy ass up here," he ordered.

"The things I'm going to do to you if you're telling the truth."

"Mmm..." I purred. "I can't wait."

"You're really here, aren't you?"

"Wait and see," I giggled, hanging up.

I checked my reflection in the mirror before heading out into the hallway. My hands were trembling as I pushed the button for the elevator. In a matter of minutes, I'd be in Oliver's arms. I knew full well of the powers he could hold over my body. Now that I was in love with him, it was going to be an entirely new sexual experience for me. I'd never made love with anyone before. It had always just been about sex.

Before I even reached Oliver's door, he opened it. Standing there in black sweatpants, he watched me approach like I was a hallucination or something. My breath hitched as I watched his hungry gaze.

"You're here," he gasped, still gawking at me.

"Why do you look so shocked?" I grinned, stepping closer toward him.

"You came all this way...for *me*?"

"I didn't want to wait two whole weeks to see you. I've waited long enough." His eyes became soft as he pulled me into his arms.

"What do you want, Jade?" he asked, running his hand through my hair, moving a stray strand from my face.

"You, Oliver. I want you," I strained. Losing every last bit of my control, I crashed my lips against his. My arms wrapped around his neck, moulding him to me as we kissed. Now that I was back in his embrace, how would I ever let him go? He responded with a groan, lifting me up in his strong arms. I heard a door close as he carried me, and realized he must have carried me to his bedroom.

"This is going to be rough at first," he snarled against my lips. He ran his hands down my body, undoing the clasps on my dress as he reached them. "I'll be softer after, I promise. Let me devour you first, please?"

"You really think I'd say no?" I panted, feeling my dress fall to the floor.

"Fuck, I love you in red," he growled, taking in my underwear before turning me around. His hands explored my body greedily, cupping my breasts while his lips attacked my neck. Reaching behind me, I wrapped my arms around his shoulders for support. "Are you ready for me?" He pushed his erection against my ass before moving his hands down into my panties. "Shit, you're so ready," he snarled, turning me around to face him. I groaned, watching him put his fingers into his mouth, tasting me. That was an Oliver trait I'd never get tired of seeing.

"Fuck, that's a taste I've missed," he moaned before lifting me off my feet carrying me to his bed. "But then my cock has missed this more." He smirked seductively, pulling my panties off with one tug before removing his sweats. Holy crap, I'd forgotten how wonderful his cock was. Arousal seeped toward my center. "Do you want this, Jade?" he groaned, stroking my folds.

"YES!" I pleaded, throwing my head back as the tip of his cock grazed my entrance.

"Do I need to wear a condom?" he suddenly stressed. I didn't want anything between us.

"No, not if you don't want to. I'm still covered. I haven't been with anyone else, either."

"I need to warn you..." he whispered, looking directly into my eyes, "I won't give up if you disappear again. I *will* find you, Jade." He meant every word he was saying. That much was clear. "I can't *ever* lose you again. If we do this now, it's for keeps."

"Oliver, I'm not going anywhere." What was I saying? It was even scarier that I believed what I was telling him.

"Promise me you'll stay."

"I promise," I beamed, leaning up to kiss him. He opened his mouth, allowing my tongue to dart in and dance with his. His hands moved up under my ass to lift my hips, and with one deep thrust, he was inside me. Feeling so full and complete after so long was pure bliss.

"Fuck!" he winced. "You're tighter than I remember."

"Ugh! It's been six months since anyone has been down there," I moaned as he pulled out and slammed back in.

"That's because this is *mine*," he growled, running his fingers over my clit. "No one can fuck you like I can!" He slammed into me harder, rotating his hips. Oh, he really was fucking me now. I fisted the bedsheets, losing my mind. All I could feel and see was him—nothing else mattered.

"O...Oh...Oliver," I rambled minutes later as he hit that special spot only he had ever found.

"Mmm," he hummed, thrusting toward that spot again. "That's what I was looking for." With the unrelentless thrusts, I was beginning to see stars. "That's it, Jade, squeeze my cock. Shit, I've missed you," he gasped, pulling my bra cups down to expose my breasts. The moment his warm mouth made contact with my left nipple I lost it, screaming out his name into the night. I felt him begin to twitch moments later, and when he did climax, it made my entire body tremble.

Oliver lay on top of me, catching his breath while I held him. I basked in his scent and the feeling of him still inside me. If this was what love felt like, I could see why people died for it. I'd never felt so connected to anyone before. From this moment on, Oliver and I would be one.

"What are you thinking?" he smirked a while later. He'd gone to the bathroom and brought back a warm washcloth, which he was gently cleaning my sex with.

"This feels so right," I groaned, running my hands into his dark hair. The things he could do with his hands. He was slowly rubbing the cloth against my clit and it felt incredible.

"Do you know what I loved about that the most?" I shook my head, frowning. "You gave into me. You didn't hold back like you used to."

"I'm not holding back any more, Oliver. You have me, you just need to be patient."

"How am I supposed to go slow when you travel halfway across the world to say things like that to me?" he scolded, shaking his head. After removing the cloth, he stroked his nose against my neck. This man knew what he was doing. I was putty in his capable hands.

"Sex has always been important between us. You know that as well as I do. We just need to take the rest slow," I stated, closing my eyes as his lips took the place of his nose.

"You're right," he muttered into the crook of my neck, arching my back so he could unhook my bra. "It's time for me to explore everything I've missed in these last six months," he smirked, making his way down my neck.

"Are you going to make me close my eyes again like the first time?" I giggled as he bit down on my nipple softly.

"Oh no, I want you to watch *everything*," he winked, looking up at me for a short second. I was going to combust.

He began to tease my nipple, rolling it between his thumb and forefinger, while squeezing my other breast, sucking my hardened peak into his mouth. I was on sensory overload. I tried to focus on the ceiling because watching him attack my breasts was too much.

"You're not watching me, Jade," he chuckled from between my breasts a moment later.

"You're driving me a little crazy here," I panted as his teeth grazed my nipples.

"That's the plan, Beautiful," he smouldered, moving lower. His fingertips and lips caressed every inch of my skin, making me squirm with desire. His lips travelled everywhere except the place I needed him most.

"Please, Oliver," I gasped as he bit gently into my inner thigh.

"I need you to turn over." *Was he being serious?* I wanted his face in between my legs, right now! "Do as I ask, Jade," he breathed, starting to roll me over. I let him, even if I was a little frustrated.

With a moan, I buried my head in the pillow as his hands moved up my legs, gripping my ass. I could feel his erection brush against my legs as he moved. Oliver hovered over me, placing soft, loving kisses on my shoulder before moving lower.

"You have the softest skin," he murmured. All I could do was answer with a groan.

I bit into the pillow when Oliver's lips traveled over my ass. He grabbed it roughly, licking across my left cheek.

"Shit," I yelled, trying hard not to move. My body was on

fire, smoldering in a pure frenzy of need. My sex was aching and drenched.

"Lift your hips. Can you get onto your knees?" he asked, his voice dripping with lust. "You can keep your head in the pillow if you want. You might need it." *Oh. My. God!* What was he going to do? I lifted my hips, raising my ass high up in the air. "Spread your legs," he ordered, using his hands to pull them apart more.

The excitement of wondering what he was going to do was making my heartbeat faster; I could feel it pulsing in my chest.

I felt Oliver shuffle around on the bed, and when his shoulders touched the inside of my thighs, I knew exactly what he was going to do.

He gripped my ass suddenly and pulled me down toward him. The moment his hot tongue met with my aching sex; I cried out in pleasure. He didn't even give me a second to recover from his sudden attack. He plunged his tongue inside me, sucking up everything he could. Holy shit! I'd forgotten how good he was at oral!

My hips were rocking against his face; I couldn't stop myself. When he began to suck my clit into his mouth, I screamed into the pillow, my orgasm hitting me out of the blue. It was one of the most intense climaxes Oliver had ever given me, and I hadn't even felt a build up.

"Oh, God," I panted, moving my head out of the pillow to look behind me. *Shit, what a sight.* Oliver was lying on his back between my legs, studying my sex. He licked his lips, tasting my arousal that was on his face.

"That's the best thing I've eaten in six months," he winked, moving out from between my legs. I thought he was going to lie down, but I was wrong. He came up behind me, circling my clit with his fingers, teasing my entrance. "I'm going to fuck you slowly now. You might want to brace yourself on the headboard," he whispered in my ear, biting my earlobe.

I gripped the headboard, using it to pull myself up slightly while he grabbed my thighs and pulled my legs apart again.

"This is my happy place," he whispered into my neck, slowly sinking himself inside me. "Everything else fades away when I'm right here." I had no words. What could I say to that?

I lost sense of time while Oliver slowly fucked me from behind. When my fingertips began to hurt from gripping the headboard too tightly, I knew we must have been making love for a while. We didn't rush our orgasms this time, though. Oliver explored my body with his hands. We were two people showing our love for each other. Tilting my head, I kissed his soft, desirable lips while I felt his cock slide in and out of me. I began meeting his thrusts when I felt myself start to build.

"Are you close?" he panted, kissing down my neck and palming my breasts in his hands.

"Ugh...yes, I'm almost there." In response, he moved one hand in between my legs and started working my clit with his fingers.

"Holy...f...fuck!" I began to fall just as his climax hit him.

"Shit, shit, shit...fuck...Jade!" His thrusts became harder as he rode out his orgasm.

We were both panting by the time it was over. I was clinging to the headboard while Oliver was clinging to my sweat covered body as we came down from our orgasms.

"Every time! Every Goddamn time, it's better than the

last," he mused, kissing my shoulder.

"Mmm," I purred, feeling him pull me down onto his chest. I couldn't stop my eyelids from closing. I was too blissfully happy to even try and stay awake.

*　*　*

My body was sore when I woke up, but in all the right places. The room was dark, but as I sat up, I noticed the blackout curtains were still closed. Having no idea what time it was, I stretched for my phone. Damn, I had really slept in. It was already afternoon. Then again, I was jetlagged.

After turning on a few lights, I searched for something to wear. Seeing one of Oliver's shirts hanging over a chair, I decided to just wear that. I suspected he was already out for the day, anyway. He must have left a note for me somewhere.

Like all the other suites he'd stayed in, this one was huge. When I wandered into the living area, I finally found a note.

> *I didn't want to wake you, Beautiful,*
> *but I'll be back around 3 pm.*
> *xxxx*

Judging by the time, Oliver would be back at any moment. I darted into the bathroom to freshen up, and by the time I came out, I could hear voices in the living area.

"Is there a reason you're changing your schedule for the rest of the week?" I had to hide my amusement at hearing Alicia's voice. Oh, she was in for a surprise when she saw me.

"It's for personal reasons. This isn't just a business trip anymore," he replied. "I need you to get me some tickets to the opera for an evening I'm free this week." Oliver was taking me to the opera? "I want the best seats."

"It's short notice, don't you think?" Alicia snapped. "Why do you need tickets for the opera, anyway?"

"Are you arguing with me, Alicia?" he fumed. "Look, I know this trip didn't go how you planned, but I'm willing to forget your outburst." What had she done now? I moved closer to the door so I could hear a little better.

"I can't help the way I feel about you," she muttered.

"Well, it's unwanted. I don't date employees and I've made that clear. More to the point, have I ever given you any reason to think I was interested in you? I rejected every advance you made toward me." At hearing his words, my heart inflated. He had turned down every opportunity to be with Alicia, even when I'd abandoned him. "I'm not disputing that you are a beautiful woman, Alicia," he soothed. I could hear her low sobs and couldn't help but roll my eyes. She was such a drama queen. "But I'm already spoken for."

"What?" Alicia gasped. "Since when?" Now seemed like it might be a good time to make myself known.

"My private life is none of your concern! But if you must know..." He was interrupted by someone else entering his suite.

"Oliver, I'm going to head to the factory with Mr. Vanzin to look at these prototypes. Would you care to join me?" It sounded like his uncle, Richard.

"Not right now, Uncle." Oliver was still angry.

"Have I interrupted something?" Richard asked.

"If you'll excuse me," Alicia whimpered. I heard the door slam moments later.

"What was all that about?" Richard asked once they were

alone. "Please don't tell me you've upset her again. Alicia is perfect for you, Oliver. Why can't you see that?" Oh great! Oliver's uncle was team Alicia. That wasn't going to help me one bit!

"I'm not you. Okay, you fell for your PA, and it worked, but I don't want to mix my private life with my business. Alicia isn't my type. I don't care if *you* think she's right for me. I know she isn't!"

"You've got to stop letting *that* woman hold you back. She's gone, Oliver." Wow! *That woman*? I could only guess Richard was talking about me.

"Don't you *dare* speak about Jade like that," Oliver snarled bitterly.

"Still, you defend her. I can't believe it!"

"You don't know the whole story."

"And you do? Oliver, she ran out on you without so much as an explanation."

"Jade is back, Uncle," Oliver muttered. Oh, I wish I could have seen Richard's face at the announcement.

"What? You found her?"

"Yes."

"Are you going to her?" Richard sounded worried.

"I don't need to." Oliver paused, and I could only assume he was trying to read Richard's face before continuing. "She's fast asleep in the next room."

"She's *here*?!"

"Yes, and I would appreciate you keeping your opinions to yourself. Jade has been back for almost five weeks. She'll hopefully be accompanying me the rest of the trip, once I've asked her."

"You never…"

"I needed time and didn't want to be influenced by you."

"Oliver, I…"

"I don't care what you think is right for me, Uncle. All I know is that I *need* Jade. Being with her these last few weeks…I feel complete again. My world isn't easy for her. She's never been around someone with my wealth before. It scared her." My heart melted at his words.

"Promise me you'll be careful. She's hurt you once, she can do it again."

"I know what I'm doing," Oliver replied sternly.

"Well, I'll send Mr. Vanzin your regards, then." I heard footsteps and a door close moments later.

I stumbled in surprise as Oliver suddenly opened the bedroom door.

"Tell me you didn't hear all that?" he winced, catching sight of me.

"So, your uncle hates me, then?" I sighed, moving to sit down on the bed.

"Don't you dare do that," he glared.

"Do what?" I frowned as he took a seat next to me on the bed.

"Start thinking of excuses to leave before we've even begun."

"Your uncle not liking me wouldn't keep me away," I grinned, leaning in to peck his lips. "I just meant it's going to get a little awkward."

Oliver's shoulders slumped. "I'm sorry. I promised I wouldn't bring up you leaving again." He ran his hands through his hair, closing his eyes.

I moved to straddle his lap, and when I did, his eyes snapped open. I was met with pure emotion gazing back at me.

"Stop apologizing...and stop worrying," I beamed, wrapping my arms around his neck while his hands found a home on my waist. "We're in this together. If anyone knows if we can make *this* work, it's us." He responded by crashing his lips to mine. We both surrendered to each other with a groan.

CHAPTER NINE

"I heard your conversation with Alicia earlier," I smirked a few hours later. We were lying in each other's arms, skin against skin, our legs all tangled together. I loved these moments almost as much as when we made love.

"Oh." Oliver looked troubled at knowing that.

"I'm not going to say anything, but I would like you to admit that I was right," I teased, running my hands down his bare chest.

"Okay," he sighed with a chuckle. "You were right."

"I want you to add my full name. You could be talking about anyone."

"Yes, Jade Gibbs, you were completely right about Alicia, my PA," he snorted, rolling on top of me and pinning me down by holding my arms above my head.

"I knew it," I giggled, trying to break free from his hold.

"I thought you weren't going to talk about it?" he questioned as his lips moved down my neck.

"What are you going to do?"

"Nothing. Alicia knows where she stands." I was trying to concentrate, but when his mouth moved toward my breasts, it became a losing battle.

"Don't you have meetings to attend?" I gasped as he grazed his lips across my ribs.

"I do, but I'm finding it hard to want to leave this bed for some reason. My uncle is taking care of my meetings, anyway."

"I didn't come to distract you, Oliver," I laughed, pushing him off me with my legs. "I came to *support* you."

"You did?" he beamed, sitting up on his knees. It was almost impossible to look away from his impressive semi-hard cock. *Jade, you have all night! Don't be a greedy bitch! Look away!* Tilting his head, he asked, "See something you like?" He was such a cocky asshole at times. *Stop thinking about cocks, too!*

"Can you stop turning every conversation we have into a discussion on sex?"

"Why? Is it making you horny?" he winked.

"I heard that you needed to talk to me about escorting you to a few events this week?" I was trying to pull this conversation out of the gutter.

"You wouldn't mind?"

"That's one of the reasons I came," I grinned, sitting up while pulling the sheet with me. "I'm here for *you*, Oliver." I stroked his face softly. He caught my hand with his when my fingertips grazed his chin.

"You have no idea what it means to hear you say that, Jade." His lips began to move toward mine, but the sound of my phone ringing made us pull away from each other.

"I have no idea who that could be," I frowned, leaning over the bed to reach it. Oh, crap! It was Georgie. She only ever called when there was an emergency. I had to answer it.

"Hello," I answered warily, looking over at Oliver.

"Please tell me the rumors I'm hearing aren't true?" Georgie snapped.

"Well, hi, Georgie. It's nice to speak to you, too," I muttered curtly, getting out of bed and wrapping the sheet around my body. Oliver was watching me intently from the edge of the mattress.

"Is he there with you now?"

"Who?" I asked with a frown.

"The Goddamn target you're in *love* with? What the hell are you playing at? How could you accept that mission?" She was fuming.

"I can't really talk right now," I stressed, turning from Oliver to look out the window.

"You are with him, aren't you?"

"Yes," I whispered.

"Jesus, Jade! What the fuck are you doing?" I could hear a male voice talking to Georgie in the background. "Yes, Drew, Molly was telling the truth. Jade, Drew wants to talk to you."

"I don't have time to talk to Drew," I sighed. "I'm in Russia right now. I have things to do. I'm not even up yet."

"We're worried about you."

"I'm fine, honest. I'll call you next week. Bye."

"You better! This chat *isn't* over," Georgie threatened before I hung up. "Sorry about that, Oliver," I mumbled, turning back to face him. "That was my friend, Georgie."

"The one married to the guy I met at the airport all those months ago? Drew, right?" Shit, I'd forgotten Oliver had met Drew.

"Yeah," I replied, joining him on the edge of the bed. "They worry about me."

"Do they know about me?"

"They know everything," I muttered. "I kept in touch with them while I was traveling."

"I tried to trace your friend Drew when you...well, you know...but it was pointless. I didn't have a last name, and I could hardly remember what he looked like. Do they still live in St. Petersburg?"

"Yeah, they do."

"How long have they been married?" How the hell should I know? They weren't even really married.

"Five years," I lied. "It was a whirlwind romance."

"I'd love to meet them some day. It will be nice to get to know some of your friends."

"They are incredibly busy. They both travel a lot," I rushed with panic in my voice.

"Jade," Oliver soothed, taking my hands in his. "I said *someday*. There's no rush. Relax."

"I'm sorry," I winced. "So, why don't you tell me about these events you need me to accompany you to?" I asked, changing the subject.

"There is a gala on Saturday, but I also have a charity event on Friday. I wouldn't mind taking you on a tour of the factory, either, to help save me from boredom."

"Boredom in a factory? I thought you were a nerd?" I teased.

"I've seen a lot of my factories, Jade. The tours are a little mundane now."

"Oh, well...in that case I'd love to. You'll have to explain all the science stuff to me, though."

"I can do that," he grinned. "And I'd be happy to take you shopping if you're worried you won't have anything suitable to wear for the gala dinner."

"Oliver, you don't have to..."

"I know I don't, but I want to." He smiled warmly, stroking the side of my face. "Let me take you shopping. Moscow has some amazing shops. Have you been to the Red Square before?" I shook my head. I'd only ever been to Moscow a few times, and I never had time for shopping. "Let me make a few calls while you have a shower and get changed."

"Oh, I'll need to call reception to get my bags from my room." Oliver grimaced. "You've already had them moved, haven't you?" I eyed him suspiciously.

"Only because I knew you'd need them when you woke up," he explained. "You don't have to stay in this suite. I'd understand if you wanted your space, I..."

"Oliver, it's fine. I want to stay here, if that's okay with you?" I interrupted.

"Of course, it is," he beamed, pecking my lips. "Alright, I'll leave you to get ready. I'll make my calls in the living area." I nodded before watching him leave.

Things were slipping back into place perfectly, but I had to remember this was a mission. As much as it pained me to be lying to Oliver in order to steal from him again, being back in his life outweighed the negative right now. He was here in front of me and I wasn't going to waste any of the time I had with him.

I was finishing off my makeup half an hour later when Oliver joined me in the bedroom again.

"I was wondering if you'd packed warm enough clothes," he chuckled, coming up behind me and placing his hands on my waist. "I don't think I've *ever* seen you with so many clothes on."

"Funny," I smirked, elbowing him in the ribs. Oliver had a point, though. I didn't usually do layers, but today I was wearing tight fitting blue jeans, a sleeveless shirt, and a thick white sweater. "Did you get all your calls done?"

"Yes, I'm all yours for the rest of the day," he beamed. *Mm… when he put it that way, did we really have to leave the hotel room?* "You've got that look on your face again," he mused. His hands were slowly creeping up into my sweater.

"What look?" I asked innocently, playing along.

"The 'I'm thinking about the amazing sex Oliver and I have' look."

"I have a look for that?" I snorted as his hands moved into my top.

"Okay, I don't like all these layers you're wearing," he smoldered into my ear. "It takes me longer to get my hands on that sexy body of yours."

"I thought we were going shopping," I giggled, squirming out of his hold. He had a playful gleam in his eyes. I raced for the living room, screaming as he chased me. "Oliver!" I screeched when he caught me around the waist. We were so involved that neither of us noticed someone had walked into the suite.

"Alicia tells me you've canceled the meeting tonight, Oliver?" Richard glared at us. "Hello, Jade," he said curtly, shooting daggers at me.

"Oh, um…hello, Richard," I stressed as Oliver and I broke apart.

"I see you've wasted no time squirming back into my nephew's life. How long are you planning on staying this time?"

"Uncle!" Oliver snapped. "You have no right to speak to Jade like that!"

"I know there is nothing I can do about this situation, but I don't have to like it!"

"But you could at least be courteous toward her!" Oliver

was losing it.

"Oliver, if that's how Richard feels, I understand," I soothed. "I have to prove myself too more than just you. Please don't let this cause friction between you and your uncle." His eyes softened as he stroked my cheek, nodding.

"And you think she isn't good for me?" Oliver mused, looking at his uncle.

"Are you expecting me and Alicia to handle your meetings while you're off gallivanting with Jade?" Richard fumed. "This is a business trip, Oliver!"

"I'm well aware of that, Richard! Jade will be accompanying me to the gala dinner and the charity event this week. I've merely postponed my meeting today. Dr. Carlton was more than happy to have a little extra time to get his notes in order. I am more than capable of running my own business *and* having the afternoon with Jade, thank you!" Watching Oliver stand up for us was turning me on so much I had to hold my legs together. Richard took one glance between us before storming off, mumbling a string of words I couldn't quite hear.

"He'll come around," Oliver soothed, pulling me into his arms. "Hey, stop with the pouty lip," he ordered, pecking my lips. I smiled at him, unable to deny him anything. "That's better. Weren't you the one who said that the only people who know we can make this work is us? It doesn't matter what he or anyone else thinks."

"I didn't come back to make life more difficult for you, though."

"Jade, Richard and I are always arguing. If it wasn't about us, it would have been something else. Now, are we going shopping or not?"

"You are so bossy," I teased, following him out of the suite.

"I've never been clothes shopping with you before. It might take the entire afternoon for you to find two dresses."

"Two?" I frowned as we made our way into the elevator.

"You won't be wearing the same dress to both events."

"Oliver, you don't have to buy me *two* dresses," I complained, crossing my arms.

"I know I don't *have* to," he chuckled, pinning me against the elevator wall. "But you've come all this way…just for me. I have to give you *something* in return."

"I think you gave me enough last night," I groaned. Even through my jeans, I could feel his erection pressing against me.

"Mm…I have no idea what you're talking about. What are you implying that I gave you last night, Jade?" he purred, leaning down to plant soft, wet kisses down my neck.

"You know very well what I'm talking about." There was no way he could have forgotten about all the sex we had last night. I playfully smacked his back when his hands gripped my ass. "Oliver," I giggled as the elevator door opened. He pulled away and when I looked around him, I came face to face with Alicia. She was standing there gawking at us.

"Oh, Alicia, you remember Jade, don't you?" Oliver said sweetly, taking my hand in his.

"From the Brentford Opening in New York, right?" Alicia glared. Oh, I could see the fury behind her eyes as she saw Oliver's hand in mine.

"Pleasure to see you again, Alicia," I grinned.

"I'm taking Jade shopping. We'll be out the entire afternoon," Oliver called, pulling me with him into the lobby area.

"She looked as if she was about to scratch my eyes out," I giggled once we were outside.

"Why do you think I pulled you out here so quickly?" he pointed out as the driver held the door open to the limo.

"You're not driving me this time?" I questioned, amused.

"Jade, we're in Moscow. I'd get us lost." He did have a point.

* * *

"What do you think? The silver one or this one?" I asked, spinning around in an elegant, deep purple, Gucci evening gown. We'd already decided on a black cocktail dress for the charity event. Now I was trying to find something for the gala.

"You look beautiful in both," he sighed, standing up. "I want you to keep that underwear on until we get back to the hotel room, too." The white lace bodice was incredibly sexy, but when I added the stockings and garters, too, I knew Oliver had a problem in his pants. It was obvious when I asked him to help me out of my last dress.

"Mm...some things never change," I purred, wrapping my arms around his neck.

"I still haven't had my fill of you yet, Jade. Not by a long shot," he whispered. "Why don't you get both the dresses? You'll get good use out of them, I promise."

"Let me buy one, then," I challenged.

"What kind of gentleman would I be if I let a lady buy her own dress? I have a reputation to uphold."

"You have to let me do *something*."

"Invite me to dinner at your new apartment when we get back to New York."

"That's it?" I frowned. I was getting a much better deal out of this.

"I just want the chance to really get to know you, Jade. I can do that better when you're surrounded by your own things. I learned so much about you in St. Petersburg all those months ago."

"Okay, deal" I sighed, turning around. "Can you help me out of this dress now, please?"

"With pleasure," he groaned, unzipping the gown before letting it fall to the ground. Oliver and I were alone in the grand changing room, and the atmosphere was fully charged. The entire room was covered in mirrors, so I couldn't miss the hungry look in his eyes as he gazed at my body. "I'm going to devour you when we get home later," he snarled, pulling my back against his chest while his hands roamed my body.

"O...oh, w...why can't we just go back now?" I pleaded, losing myself in his touch.

"I have one more place I want to take you," he whispered into the crook of my neck, biting gently. "Then we'll have an early night, I think. Dinner in bed."

"Ugh...sounds perfect," I panted.

"But, right now, I'll let you get dressed before I take you right in this changing room."   Hell, I'd let Oliver fuck me right now, but of course shy Jade...well, that wasn't her style.

"I think that's a good idea," I giggled, forcing a blush.

He grinned, turning me around to peck my lips. "I'll wait for you outside." I nodded, a little dizzy when he finally let me go. "Oh, and Jade," he called just before leaving, "I meant what I said about the underwear. Keep it on. I'll clear it with the shop assistant right now."

There went the waterfall between my legs again. *Damn you, Oliver!*

CHAPTER TEN

"Oliver," I gasped, taking everything in. "I don't know what to say."

"Is this too much?" he questioned, uncertain. We had the Pushkin Museum of Fine Art all to ourselves. It was supposed to be closed, but he had somehow managed to get us in after normal business hours.

"Do you know how many artists are on display here? Van Gogh, Gauguin, Picasso, Dufrénoy, and Matisse—just to name a few. Oh. My. God! The *La Vigne Rouge* is here!" I squealed excitedly.

"The what?" he chuckled.

"The Red Vineyard by Van Gogh," I glared. "You know that painting, right?"

"Can't say that I do. I'm a science nerd, remember? I don't really know that much about artwork."

"Then I need to educate you," I snorted, dragging him inside the museum.

"I could watch you gazing at these paintings all night," Oliver murmured into my ear while he stood behind me.

"How did you manage to get us in here after closing time, anyway?" I questioned, turning to wrap my arms around his neck. "Did you bribe security? I didn't even know you could speak Russian," I teased, nudging him playfully.

"I think it's more about Russia trying to bribe *me*," he chuckled, shaking his head from a sudden thought. I couldn't help but notice the humor in his eyes dull for a few seconds. Russia was trying to bribe Oliver? *Why?* Then it dawned on me... Did they want his machine? Was I working for Russia?

"You know I have no idea what you're talking about, right?" I frowned, running my fingertips across the back of his neck.

"You will by the end of this trip with me. You're going to be meeting *a lot* of my associates over the next few days."

"Why would Russia be bribing you?" I frowned, acting dumb.

"Why do you think?" He smiled sadly, stroking my cheek as he looked into my eyes. "My uncle insisted on this trip. He wants us to strengthen our relationship with the military here."

"Are you going to sell them your machines?"

"Not if I can help it," he sighed, taking my hand in his and intertwining our fingers.

"I remember you telling me that you only do business with certain countries."

"I'm impressed," he grinned.

"Is Russia a country you don't like to do business with?" I asked, interested.

"Russia isn't part of NATO, which can complicate things. My father always warned me against them, Israel, and Japan. I know it's wrong to judge some countries from their past...but..."

"You don't have to explain yourself to me. You're a wise man, Mr. Kirkham. I knew that the moment I met you."

"Really?" His eyes widened. "And how did you know that?"

"You had everyone in that bar eating out of your hands.

I'd never seen anyone control a room the way you did. Everyone hangs on your every word."

"Mm...does that include you?" he smoldered, pulling me flush against his strong chest.

"You know it does," I panted, placing my hand over his heart.

"What if I told you I wanted to fuck you in this museum... with all these paintings watching us?" *Oh crap!* There went another pair of panties. Why did that sound so wrong, but also right at the same time?

"I think that would end up in us getting arrested," I groaned, trying to break free from his hold.

He chuckled, letting me go. "Maybe you're right. How about dinner here instead?" Was he being serious?

"You can't bring food into a museum like this. Do you have any idea how valuable these paintings are?"

"I wasn't planning on throwing my food at them, were you?" He grinned mischievously. He was so damn cocky!

"There is no way the museum would allow us to eat in here," I pointed out.

"Are you sure about that?" he questioned, taking a step back, silently beckoning me to follow him.

"Yes," I glared before my eyes fell upon a candlelit table set up for two. He was such a show off! "What the hell?" I gasped. "Oliver...how...when..." I was gobsmacked.

"Let's take a seat, Jade," he chuckled, pulling me toward the table. "Would you like some wine?" I nodded, looking around. We were completely alone. Where had all the security guards gone? When I turned back to where he was leading me, I noticed a large, covered serving dish in the center of the table.

"I've spared no expense on dinner tonight," he grinned, pouring us both a glass of white wine.

"I can't believe you've managed to do this."

"Do you like it?"

"Oliver, I *love* it!"

"Good," he beamed, lifting the cover off the serving dish.

"Pizza?" I snorted. "My, you really did go all out."

"I didn't want to go too over the top. This is me taking things slowly." I could actually see his logic. Everything was perfect.

The pizza was really good, not to mention the company. I fell a little more in love with him while we sat eating, surrounded by Van Gogh, Gauguin, Picasso, Dufrénoy, and Matisse. Oliver knew the real *me* so well. How was that even possible?

✳ ✳ ✳

"How would you rate that as a date?" he asked in the back of the limo as we headed back to the hotel.

"One of the best I've *ever* had." I scooted closer to him so I could rest my head on his shoulder. He draped his arm around me and we sat in a comfortable silence until we reached the hotel.

"So nice of you to show your face, Oliver," Richard glared as we entered his suite. "I was starting to wonder if you'd ever make it back."

"I told you; I cleared my schedule for the rest of the day. Jade and I needed to make sure she had the right attire for the charity event and gala."

"Have you even checked your messages?" Richard fumed. Oliver frowned, looking down at his phone. "Don't worry, Oliver. I'll run your company for you while you make a complete fool of yourself again."

"Excuse us for just a moment, Jade," Oliver soothed, trying to compose himself before turning toward his uncle. "Let's take this conversation out on the balcony, Uncle," he seethed. This was going to be bad. I could tell by the fury in Oliver's eyes.

I tried hard not to listen to their confrontation, but they were both shouting so loud.

"Why can't you just be happy for me?" Oliver pleaded.

"That *woman* is running circles around you. A man like you can't be in that position. If your father..."

"Don't you *dare* bring him into this!"

"Oliver, why can't you see what a mistake you are making? Alicia..."

"Will you stop trying to interfere in my personal life? I know what I want."

"I don't think you do. You really think Jade will fit into your world? Do you really think she is strong enough? She ran scared before."

"Why are you doing this?" The pain in Oliver's voice was clear.

"I'm trying to make you see what is right in front of you. With Alicia by your side, you would be unstoppable. You know that girl is madly in love with you, don't you? You've been so clouded by your feelings for Jade, but Oliver, open your eyes! Alicia is a strong, intelligent, beautiful woman. She is just what you need. *She'll* help you to succeed in this world, not Jade!" I put my hands on the wall in front of me, shaking my head. Alicia was *not* what Oliver needed. Richard had described me, too. Well, the real Jade, that is.

"Uncle, you need to stop this. You will only push me farther away. I'm in love with *Jade*. She. Is. What. I. Want!" I closed my eyes when hearing his words. Okay, so I was on the other side of the wall, but Oliver had just said he still loved me. My heart swelled deep in my chest.

"Then you're a fool!" Richard spat before storming off.

"It would seem I have some work to do with your uncle," I sighed, walking out onto the balcony a few moments later. Oliver was leaning against the wall, watching Moscow come to life as the sun started to set.

"He is so stubborn! He thinks he knows everything! I don't have to listen to him, though. He's just my Goddam lawyer. He has no real hold on me or my business," Oliver stressed, pushing off the wall and turning to me. "I'm not making a mistake, am I? Please tell me he isn't right? I'm so blinded by you, Jade. I'm not sure I can trust my feelings when I can't even see straight." The turmoil on his face was excruciating to watch.

How many more times could I lie to him? The truth was, I didn't know what our future held, but deep inside my heart, I knew all I wanted was him.

"I know I haven't been truthful, and I have kept things from you, but believe me when I say this...all I've ever wanted is *you*." His eyes blazed with elation, and in one swift move, I was up in his arms as his lips crashed against mine.

"Shit, Jade," he moaned against my mouth, pulling my sweater over my head. "You're wearing too many damn clothes." I giggled against his lips as I began to rid him of his sweater and shirt, too.

"It gives me longer to get you naked," I purred, pulling on his bottom lip with my teeth. I needed to rein myself back in. I was being a little too bold for shy Jade.

"Oh, it's a race now, is it?" he smoldered, undoing the buttons on my jeans. "You know I'll always win. Fuck, you *did* keep the underwear on from our shopping trip." He groaned, cupping my breasts. I could tell from the look in his eyes that I was in trouble. "Do you have any idea how sexy you are?"

I shook my head, stepping out of my jeans as they hit the floor. "Maybe you should show me?" I suggested with a playful smirk. Oliver pounced, throwing me over his shoulder and carrying me to the bed.

"You want me to show you how sexy you are, huh?" he smoldered into my ear, peeling the rest of my clothes and underwear off. "Well, we'll need a mirror for that." This guy was a sex God! He could be a damn Seductor with all these tricks.

"A mirror?" I widened my eyes, acting shocked as he moved the free standing, long mirror to the side of the bed.

"Go and lie on your stomach in front of the mirror." Of course I did as he asked. I loved the way he took charge. It was a refreshing change for me. Being a Seductor, I usually held all the cards. Oliver came up behind me, his hands instantly roaming up my legs, stroking over my butt. "I need you on all fours, Beautiful, and make sure you look at your reflection in the mirror," he murmured once his hands had explored me.

"You're really going to make me watch myself, while you… while you're…"

"While I fuck you from behind? Yes," he winked in the mirror, helping me get onto my hands and knees. "Can you see how sexy you are now?" he questioned, running his fingers in between my legs, right inside my core. "Look at yourself, Jade. You're a goddess." I looked up, watching myself while he began a frantic pace with his fingers. "You must be able to see that?" I couldn't really focus on anything—only his fingers sliding in and out of me. "Maybe you'll see it more with my cock inside you. Would you like that? Do you want to watch me fuck you from behind?" All I could do was give a low groan, gripping the comforter as I became even wetter. "Oh, you like the sound of that, don't you?" he purred, circling his fingers around my clit. "You know I can't resist pleasing you. If that's what you want, then that's what you're going to get!" With his last word, he penetrated me deeply.

"Oh fuck!" I cried out.

"You haven't seen anything yet, Baby." Oliver began to pound into me, holding my hips to keep me steady. "Keep looking in that mirror. If you drop your eyes, I'll stop," he ordered.

Watching him fuck me from behind with such carefree lust was like a catalyst that set off my orgasm. He was watching his cock slide in and out of me, glancing every now and then into the mirror to make sure I was still watching him. "Can you see how sexy you are now? Can you see what you do to me? You drive me crazy!" he gasped, thrusting deeper and harder.

"Ugh...yes!"

"You are so fucking sexy."

"O...Oliver...deeper!" I was building quickly.

"Are you going to cum all over my cock, Beautiful? I. Want. It. Right. Now!" At his words and the feeling of his fingers running over my clit, I came, screaming toward the mirror as I watched myself come undone. Jesus, I did look hot when I orgasmed.

"Did you enjoy that?" he chuckled as I collapsed onto his chest from exhaustion.

"I don't deserve all these orgasms," I yawned, pulling myself closer to him.

"Oh, yes you do, and I've only just started with you, but for tonight…sleep. Tomorrow is a new day." I closed my eyes at his words, secure in his loving arms but excited with what was to come.

✳ ✳ ✳

"I can't believe you had the nerve to show up here," Alicia seethed from across the table. Oliver had already left for the morning to attend an important meeting.

"You really thought you'd win this mission, didn't you?" I snorted, sipping my coffee. "It's over, Alicia. Oliver is *my* target!"

"That doesn't mean you'll complete this assignment. You may be back in his bed, but this case is impossible."

"To you, maybe, but if this power core *is* real, I'll find it."

"You really think you're something, don't you?" she yelled with pure hatred in her voice.

"Compared to you, yes," I admitted. "You're disloyal. You would have stolen your target's money if I'd given you half the chance last year."

"You had no right to interfere! It wasn't your mission! You were just the surveillance."

"I never turned you in, Alicia. You should be thanking me." Looking back now, I wish I had informed Sonia of Alicia's plan. She'd have been thrown out of the Seductors for it. Then again, I was worried she'd have a far worse fate. I couldn't be responsible for anyone's death—not again.

"If I had been given some of the assignments you were given, I wouldn't have needed the money!" Now I was getting the truth.

"You need to watch that greed. It will consume you and be your downfall one day," I stated. "You earn more than enough. All Seductors do!"

"I don't need to sit and listen to this shit," she snarled, standing up to storm off.

"Oh, Alicia," I suddenly remembered. "Are you going to send Sonia a progress report? Or do you want me to?" I grinned sarcastically.

"Fuck you, Jade," she spat, slamming the door behind her. *Okay, I guess I have to do it.*

Once I'd written the report and sent it over, my phone rang. I wasn't shocked that Sonia called me.

"Is now a good time to talk?" she asked when I answered after the second ring.

"Yes, I'm alone." I stretched, standing to walk around the large suite.

"I knew you'd do it, Jade. It took you no time at all."

"Now that I have this mission, will you be drawing up a written agreement about your deal?"

"That's what I'm calling for. Your agreement is being drawn up as we speak. I'll send you over a copy once it's done. You can sign next month when you come back to headquarters for your six month training."

"You make it sound so easy. How would I even explain a three year disappearance? He might not even wait for me."

"I've already thought about that. We'll add in a kidnap situation." What? "You'll be taken along with the power core, if it exists." That was crazy talk! "You'll be released after three years, when we let Oliver track you."

"Sonia, that's insane!"

"Do you have a better suggestion?" Damnit! I really didn't. I wanted something as undramatic as possible for Oliver, but how would that work? I was going to be gone for *three years.* "We have time, Jade. It was just an idea."

"What's going to happen to Alicia now that I've taken control of this mission?" I wanted her on a plane as soon as possible.

"We're keeping you both in play until you've discovered which scientist Mr. Kirkham is working with on the core. We may fake an illness for a few months if Alicia is needed on another mission, but she might be put to good use if it's a male." Now I was pissed! I didn't *want* Alicia on this mission.

"Is that really necessary? You know I can handle both."

"I'm aware of that, Jade, but this mission is too important to take any risks. You'll have to put up with her a little longer."

"Great," I sighed. "She's going to try and sabotage my mission, Sonia. She's already made a few attempts. Can you at least fake an illness sooner rather than later? I need time to gain Oliver's trust back, and Alicia being here won't help that. You can bring her back in on the case when I have more information," I pleaded. Sonia was quiet on the other end of the line. "Please?" I whispered.

"Oh, okay," she huffed. "I'll try and get her assigned to a few smaller missions as soon as I can."

"Away from New York?" I added.

"Yes," Sonia chuckled. "Now, you get to work. I want a new progress report by the end of the week." With that, she hung up.

I was still checking over my dresses when Oliver finally got back an hour later.

"How was your morning, Dear?" I grinned, turning around to look at him.

"Busy," he sighed, loosening his tie away and collar. "How was your morning?"

"Lonely," I pouted, falling into his waiting arms. "Your PA stopped by to visit me."

"Why?" he frowned, leaning down to plant a soft, chaste kiss on my lips.

"I think she was just trying to weigh up the competition." I giggled as his hands glided down my back.

"There is no competition," he murmured, grazing his lips against my mouth. My body was already convulsing with need for him.

"What time do we need to leave for the charity event?" I asked innocently, wrapping my arms around his neck.

"In about three hours." His eyes became hungry as he captured my lips with a deep kiss. His hands moved down my back until they were gripping my ass. "How did I manage to last without you for six months?" he groaned, kissing his way down my neck, licking and sucking as he went. "Fuck, Jade, now that you're here, I want you *all* the time."

"You have me, Oliver. I want you as much as you want me," I panted as he pushed me against the wall. *Wall sex with Oliver! Yes, I remember that!*

"I've been daydreaming about fucking you all morning. I was sitting in my meeting, thinking about your naked body under mine," he cooed into my ear, undoing the buttons on my jeans. "It certainly made my meeting go quicker." He smirked, slipping his hands into my panties. I was at his mercy, lost in the feel of his fingers rubbing my clit softly. "Oh, Beautiful, I love how your body reacts to my touch."

"Oliver, please," I pleaded, needing more. Before I could blink, my sweater was being pulled over my head and he was attacking my breasts with his mouth, pulling the cups of my bra down as he greedily suckled each one in turn.

"I hope you're ready for this," he winked, looking up at me as he pulled my panties down. He then undid his slacks, freeing his leaking cock. *I was always ready!*

He slammed into me hard, so much that my head hit the wall. It was only a little bump, and I was too lost in the pleasure to give a shit about the slight pain anyway.

Both his hands were holding my legs up as he rolled his hips and began to really fuck me. His pace was frantic. My legs wrapped around his waist, drawing him even closer. I'd forgotten how much I loved being fucked this way. I wasn't shocked when I began to build, my orgasm rising to the surface.

"Wait for me, Beautiful," he panted. "I'm almost there." I tried, I really did, but like everything that involved Oliver, I couldn't control myself. I cried out his name as I came hard, drowning in pure bliss. He followed moments later.

"Sorry," I gasped immediately. "I couldn't hold on."

"That's okay, we have lots of time to practice," he grinned, running his hand through my hair before looking at his watch. "In fact, we still have time now." Without warning, I was thrown over his shoulder as he carried me to the bedroom.

I loved this side of Oliver so much. Oh, who was I kidding?

I loved everything about him. The problem was, did I let him know that yet?

CHAPTER ELEVEN

"You look stunning, Jade," Oliver gasped when I entered the living room in my black cocktail dress. *Oh. My. God!* Oliver in a tux. There were no words to describe how good he looked. I stood there gawking at him. I must have looked like I was catching flies. Fighting the real me that wanted to jump his *fine* bones, I composed myself.

"You look rather dashing yourself." I smiled shyly, playing with my purse. Avoiding eye contact was a good idea while I reigned in wild Jade.

"I love what you've done with your hair," he whispered from right in front of me. Closeness wasn't the best thing right then, but I managed as best I could. I'd curled my hair in soft ringlets, and put one side up using a deep red rose clip.

"Thank you." I gazed up at him. Desire pulsed through my veins as his hooded eyes met with mine. How could two people have this level of sexual need for each other? We'd only finished our last love making session an hour ago. It was there, though. Oliver wanted me again.

"We better get moving," he coughed, trying to break our connection. "Duncan will be waiting for us." I nodded, allowing him to help me into my coat before leading me out into the hallway.

"So, what is this charity event for?" I asked once we were

in the limo.

"Cancer Research. I work quite closely with some of the biggest contributors. What those scientists could achieve with the right tools is astonishing."

"You are amazing," I sighed, overcome by his statement. "Have you always been so generous?"

"To causes that matter, yes. My father always said that with wealth comes great responsibility. You have to put it back in the right places. Okay, I make money out of selling nuclear machines and weapons, but I put it back into the charities that matter—the ones that affect the whole world." He was so open with me, and it hurt that I couldn't return the favor. I wanted Oliver to love the *real* me, too!

"Will you be giving a speech tonight?"

"Only a small one. I'll probably have to draw a few times for the raffle and hand out some prizes, though."

"You take everything in your stride, don't you?"

"Why do you say that?" he questioned, his eyes roaming down my leg. Oliver and I in the back of a limo often ended one way. I couldn't afford for that to happen right now, though—not after I'd spent so long getting ready.

"I couldn't get up in front of hundreds of strangers like you can."

"It's all about practice. I've been doing public speaking since I was a boy. It was something my father insisted on."

"Your father sounds like he was very strict when you were a child."

"He was, but loving, too. I knew he only wanted the best for me."

"My dad wasn't strict at all." I put my hand over my mouth

as soon as the words slipped out. Shit! Did I really just say that out loud? I never spoke about my family to anyone.

"It's okay, Jade. You don't have to say anything else if you don't want to," Oliver whispered, stroking my hair before twisting one of my curls around his finger. "It's enough for now that you even mentioned him to me."

"He doesn't care about me anymore. Can we just leave it at that for now?"

"Of course we can." He smiled sadly, leaning down to kiss my lips. I could feel his unspoken words in that simple gesture. It was soft yet passionate. He was trying to tell me I didn't need to worry about my family. That he cared for me and that was all that mattered. If he knew the truth about my past, though, I'm not so sure he would still think that way.

We had pulled up outside the Moscow Grand Hotel when we finally broke from our kiss. "Are you ready for this?" he winked as Duncan opened the door for us.

"I can't wait." He took my hand to help me out of the car.

Watching Oliver work a crowd could never bore me. He was a well educated man—I knew that—but he had the gift of conversation. There wasn't a single topic he couldn't talk about. He could switch from nuclear warfare to the best live bands he's seen, all in a matter of seconds.

"Have you really seen that many live concerts?" I asked as we stood at the bar.

"I went through a phase of watching as many live bands as I could."

"Do you go through phases a lot?" I teased. "Are you one of those people who buy exercise machines and never use them?"

"I own a gym in New York, Jade. I use it almost every

day, remember?" Hot, sweaty Oliver. How could I have forgotten that?

"Oliver!" a male voice called. I turned to see a tall, elegant, fair-haired man standing behind me. "I told you I'd make it."

"It's good to see you, Dylan," Oliver grinned, shaking his hand. "It's so good of you to come. I know how busy you are."

"You're the boss. If you tell me to take a break, I take a break," he chuckled, turning his eyes to me. "And who is this lovely lady?"

"This is Jade Gibbs," Oliver introduced. "Jade, this is a friend of mine, Dr. Dylan Reynolds." I instantly recognized the name from the list of possible scientists working on the power core.

"It's a pleasure to meet you, Dr. Reynolds." I smiled shyly as he took my hand and kissed my knuckles.

"Call me Dylan," he smirked, looking toward Oliver. "You finally found her again then?"

"Jade found me, actually," Oliver chuckled, pulling me gently into him.

"I'm happy for you both. Macy will be thrilled, too. She was so worried about you, Oliver."

"Is Macy here?" he stressed, his hands dropping from my waist. Macy? Who the hell was that?

"Yeah, she wanted to come," Dylan frowned. "Is that a problem?" Before Oliver could respond, a female appeared behind Dylan. She had a thin, agile body, deep black hair, and big brown eyes.

"Oliver Kirkham," she sighed with her hands on her hips. "You look *so* much better. Have you finally gotten over that idiot of a woman that left you?" She flung her arms around him while

I, the 'idiot of a woman,' stood watching them. "You look good, Handsome. Really good," she mused, stroking his jacket. Okay, now she needed to let him go! I still had a damn stun gun in my purse!

"Macy," Oliver laughed nervously, turning to me with an apologetic look as he pulled away from her. "I'd like you to meet *Jade*." Realization hit her face as she looked at me.

"Jade?" she questioned. "As in *the* Jade?"

"Yep, I'm the idiot of a woman that left him. It's nice to meet you, Macy," I glowered, holding my hand out to her.

"Holy crap! I'm so sorry, Jade," she gasped as Oliver and Dylan began to laugh. "It's a pleasure to meet you, really."

"I'm sure," I muttered, relaxing when I felt Oliver's arms around me again.

"It's my fault. Macy is a *very* old friend of mine. I hadn't had the chance to tell her that I'd found you again."

"You could have picked up the phone, Oliver," Macy scolded. "I know you're a busy CEO, but it was *one* damn call!"

"Macy is an amazing scientist like Dylan," Oliver responded, ignoring her comment. "They work in Kirkham Industries' Fusion Department near Macon." He seemed to really ponder his next choice of words. "She and I went to high school together." Judging by the uncomfortable tone in his voice, I knew what was coming next. "We dated for a while, too."

"A *while*," Macy snorted. "It was *all* of High School, Oliver. We even lasted almost a year in college." I tried to fight the jealousy. Macy had dated Oliver a long time ago—it was all in the past—but why was she working for him? Looking at her, she was totally the opposite of me. She shared his interests and wasn't lying about who she really was. Macy was everything that Oliver needed. That didn't mean that I would ever give him up, though. I was too selfish for that.

"Oh, so you two were childhood sweethearts?" I mumbled, downing the rest of my wine. The room suddenly felt stifling. Oliver nodded, looking down at me.

"Excuse me. I need a little air. This wine is going to my head," I muttered, starting to move away. Oliver grabbed my arm gently, stopping me in my tracks.

"Do you want me to escort you outside?" he asked worriedly.

"I won't be long. You stay with your friends," I breathed, walking away as he let me go.

I braced myself against the wall outside the hotel, breathing in the fresh air. What the hell was happening to me? I was overcome with emotion because I'd met someone Oliver had dated in *high school*. It was ridiculous.

I had no reason to be worried. He wanted *me*—he'd already proven that—but what would happen when I left again? Would he turn to Macy for comfort? When my contract with the Seductors was over, would I find out that Macy had already taken my place? Why was I even worrying about that now? I was nowhere near completing my mission yet.

"Jade," Oliver's concerned voice broke me from my thoughts. "Are you alright?"

"Yeah," I smiled weakly. "I'm sorry. I drank my wine too quickly. It made me a little dizzy."

"Why don't you take a seat? I'll sit with you for a while," he suggested, motioning to the table and chairs behind us.

"No, you have a charity event to attend. You can't stay out here with me," I complained, letting him guide me over to the comfortable, cushioned chairs.

"You know there is no place I'd rather be than right here with you," he whispered, taking my hands in his once we both sat down. "Macy means nothing to me, Jade."

"Oliver, you don't have to…"

"I know I don't have to explain myself," he interrupted. "But I want to. Macy may have been my perfect match mentally in my early years, but it was never enough. I needed more."

"More of what?" I was acting dumb; I knew exactly what he meant.

"This," he sighed, running his fingers down the inside of my arms before gripping my wrists gently. My body began to shudder at his simple touch and an ache was building between my legs. "The connection I have with you, Jade…I can't even put it into words. You give me everything I've been searching for—you give me a home. My life with *you* means everything." He always had a way to render me speechless. "Am I getting too heavy? Tell me and I'll back off." The fear in his eyes tore me in two. I'd made Oliver doubt having strong feelings for me when I walked out on him. How I wished I could put the Seductors behind me and move on into this new life with him, but that was impossible. I had to salvage this situation as best as I could. Somehow, I had to make this work so we could have a future one day.

"You're not pushing too much," I whispered, moving to slide onto his lap. His arms automatically wrapped around me. "I can feel the connection, too." I leaned down, capturing his lips with mine. We both groaned at the taste of each other as our tongues began to dance at a slow, sensual pace. I gripped the back of his chair, crashing my body against his strong chest as his hands began to run up legs.

"Beautiful, we need to stop before I fuck you right here," he panted. His lips were moving hungrily down my neck.

"Okay," I giggled as I tried to pull away, but he held me close.

"You have no idea what it means to me to have you here. Thank you."

"I wanted to be here," I smiled, pecking his lips when he released his arms from around me. "Now, let's go back to talk to your high school crush," I winked, holding my hand out to help him up. Oliver snorted, shaking his head at me before taking my hand. With his arm tightly around me, he escorted me back into the hotel.

"Aren't we going back to talk with Macy and Dylan?" I frowned at Oliver as we headed in the opposite direction from them.

"Not right now. I think it's better if we mingle for a while."

"I'm okay. It was just the initial shock, I promise. I didn't think I'd be meeting one of your ex-girlfriends tonight—that's all."

"I wasn't expecting Macy to be here. I thought she'd stay in Macon. Parties aren't usually her thing." Macy still lived in her childhood home. Was that to be closer to Oliver? Now I was being stupid—he spent most of his time in New York, not Macon.

"Did you hire her, or did Dylan?" I suddenly thought. Was there more to their relationship?

"Macy is an amazing Nuclear Physicist. I'm lucky to have her on my team."

"So *you* hired her?" Why did that hurt so much?

"Not for the reason you're thinking," he muttered, raising

his eyebrows. "It has nothing to do with our past. It's all about her work ethic with Dylan. You can't imagine the things they are capable of." Actually, I could, but he didn't know that. Was Dylan or Macy the scientist I was looking for? Could it be that easy? I had no proof, but it was a start.

"Now you're losing me," I giggled, taking the glass of wine he was offering me.

"It's okay, Jade," he chuckled. "You don't have to understand everything."

"You mean I can just stand here and look pretty?" I teased. "Like some trophy girlfriend?"

"I wasn't aware we'd gotten to that stage so quickly." Oliver's eyes lightened with humor as he pulled me against him. "Were you even my *girlfriend* before?" Talk about me putting my foot in my mouth. Why did he have that effect on me?

"I…um…I…"

"I'm teasing you, Beautiful," he grinned, leaning down to peck my lips before escorting me back into the crowd to mingle some more.

❊ ❊ ❊

By the end of the evening, I'd met so many people that their names and faces were blurring into one.

Oliver was busy saying goodbye to a few of his guests when I suddenly needed to use the restroom. I'd had a lot of wine tonight, and I was honestly shocked I hadn't needed to go sooner.

I was touching up my makeup in the mirror when Macy walked in. Oh, this wasn't good.

"I've been trying to get you alone all night," she stated, joining me at the sinks to wash her hands.

"You have?" I frowned, turning to face her.

"If you hurt him again, I'll be coming after you."

"Excuse me?" I choked. Had I just been threatened by a science nerd?

"You didn't see him when you left. You broke that man in two!" Oliver was comforted by Macy, his ex? *Jade, cool it. You'll break character!*

"You know nothing about Oliver and me. This is none of your business!" I glared, starting to storm off.

"He's my friend!" she yelled, yanking my arm back. "This has *everything* to do with me!"

"Get the hell off me!" I seethed, pulling my arm back.

"I've seen your type around him before. I can't believe he is actually falling for your act."

"Don't think for one second that you know me, Macy," I threatened. She couldn't be any closer to the truth, but there was no way she could know who I really was.

"If you're after his money, he'll work it out. He's done it before."

"I don't want his money," I spat. "All I want is him." Macy's eyes widened in shock at my statement. "Think what you'd like of me. All I give a shit about is Oliver's opinion." With that, I stormed off. I'd broken character a little in that confrontation, but I couldn't help it.

Oliver was searching the crowd as I walked out, and when our eyes met, he instantly relaxed.

"I needed to use the restroom, sorry," I giggled as he reached me. "You were busy with your guests. I didn't want to interrupt."

"You can always interrupt me, Beautiful," he beamed, pulling me into his arms. "Are you ready to leave?" I nodded, looking back at Macy as she exited the restroom.

"Goodnight, Oliver—Jade," Macy muttered, walking past us. Oliver barely had time to respond before she left.

"What was that all about with Macy?" Oliver asked, helping me into my coat in the lobby.

"She confronted me in the restroom," I whispered.

"She did what?" he fumed. "Jade, I'm so sorry. First my uncle, now..."

"They care about you. Don't be angry with them," I sighed, stroking his face. Oliver leaned into my touch, closing his eyes.

"Let's get back to the hotel. I just want to be alone with you. Nothing makes more sense to me than that." I had to agree; even *I* could forget everything when we were connected intimately.

❋ ❋ ❋

"I'm impressed," I giggled, watching Oliver stalk toward me as we entered the bedroom. "You managed to keep your hands to yourself in the limo."

"That's because I knew I'd have you all alone soon enough," he purred, unbuttoning his shirt. I wasn't sure what was sexier—a *naked* Oliver, or watching him *get* naked.

My eyes were drawn to the well defined 'V' as he undid his slacks. Unable to hide my desire, I licked my lips and began to unzip my dress.

"What do you think you're doing?" he questioned,

stepping out of his pants when they hit the floor.

"Taking my dress off," I frowned. "Isn't that the idea? We both get naked."

"The only person stripping you tonight will be me," he ordered with a playful look in his eyes. I felt a gush of wetness between my legs. *Oh, Oliver wanted to play!*

"Mmm..." I dropped my hands, watching him move toward me. "I like that idea."

"I thought you would," he whispered, stepping up behind me. Slowly, he unzipped my dress, his fingertips grazing the bare part of my back as the zipper moved lower and lower. Pushing the dress off my shoulders, it finally fell to the floor. "There are so many positions I want to fuck you in right now that I can't even pick one," he groaned. His hands began gliding up my back slowly. My body moved on its own accord, leaning against his strong, bare chest. "Maybe I'll pick a few. Would you like that, Beautiful?"

"Ugh! Yes, fuck me anyway you like," I pleaded, groaning as his hands traveled around my ribs and slipped inside my bra, rolling and pulling on my hardening nipples.

Oliver took that as an invitation. The next thing I knew, he had me bent over the couch, gripping the cushions for support as he pulled my panties down. His talented fingers moved into my slick folds, and I groaned into the couch, knowing it would drive him crazy to see how much I wanted him already.

"Jesus, Jade!" he snarled, parting my legs a little more with his free hand. "You're so goddamn wet!" He teased my entrance, rubbing his cock against my clit. His actions only made me wetter.

"Please," I pleaded. "Please, Oliver!" I'd never begged with a man to fuck me before, but Oliver was different. For one, I was in love with him, but it was more than that. He could bring me to life. He made me forget why I was here when he controlled me this way.

"It's okay, Beautiful." His voice was laced with need. "You're getting all of this, I promise. I'm just getting you as *wet* as I can so I can pound the fuck out of you." *Oh, God!* I was sure he could make me cum just with his voice if he kept talking that way. "Oh, you like that," he mused, slowly rubbing the tip of his cock against my entrance. I pushed back against him, trying to draw him inside me, but the bastard pulled back. He was such a tease. "Maybe I should make you beg a little more first? How much do you want this, Jade?"

"For fuck's sake, Oliver! Just FUCK ME!" There went the real me, breaking free for a split second. She got her way, though, as he thrust deep inside me. The couch was sliding around because his thrusts were so hard. Gripping the arm of the couch, I held on for dear life as he fucked me from behind.

"Is this what you wanted?" he panted between thrusts. His hands were gripping my hips as he pounded into me over and over again.

"Y...yes," I groaned, trying to lift my head up but the intense orgasm was already beginning to rise to the surface.

"That's it. Jade. Give it all to me." His hands snaked around to my clit, and with three flicks of his fingers, I was lost.

Intense Oliver orgasms were the best thing—ever!

CHAPTER TWELVE

Waking up in Oliver's arms after a long night of lovemaking—happiness was an understatement. I turned my head to gaze at him sleeping peacefully beside me. He had one arm wrapped around my waist, holding me to him, and I didn't feel suffocated in his embrace. It felt like I was finally home.

I studied his face, tracing every line with my eyes. He was too perfect for words. Even with his crazy sex hair.

"You better not be watching me sleep." His lips twitched into a smirk, but his eyes stayed closed. How did he know I was looking at him?

"If you're talking to me, you're not really asleep," I giggled, snuggling into him as he pulled me even closer.

"True," he chuckled, finally opening his eyes. I would never tire of his hypnotizing brown, almost black eyes, gazing into the depths of my very soul. It was almost as if he was searching for the real Jade trapped inside. If anyone would ever be able to free the real Jade—the Jade *before* the Seductors—it would be him. "Good Morning, Beautiful," he sighed, inhaling my skin. "How did you sleep?"

"Fine, once you stopped molesting me," I teased.

"Oh, you loved every minute of it. Don't even try to deny it," he chuckled, nipping at my neck. "I could molest you again right now, if you wanted."

"No you can't. You have meetings to attend. I need to get in your uncle's good graces again, remember?" I pointed out.

Oliver froze against my neck, groaning. "But I'd rather stay right here with you," he whispered in my ear. "The world outside can wait. Now that I've got you back, I don't want to waste a moment."

"I'll still be here when you get back. Plus, it's the gala tonight." Oliver looked over at his nightstand, checking the time.

"Jesus, I've slept for seven hours," he gasped, looking down at me.

"That's because of all the fantastic sex last night," I winked. "You wore us both out." He looked at me smugly. *Oh, Oliver, trust me…I could wear you out in half the time if I was given the chance.*

"Can you call reception for some coffee and toast while I jump in the shower?" he asked, darting out of bed.

"Sure," I smiled, stretching for the phone while watching his sexy, naked butt walk into the bathroom.

Half an hour later, Oliver was downing his cup of coffee while wearing a stylish, navy blue suit. "I'll be in meetings until this evening. Alicia will see that you get to the gala. I'll be meeting you there."

"What about your tux?" I asked.

"I'm having it delivered to the event. I'll get changed there. What are you planning to do with your day?"

"I'm going to roll around in these sheets for the first few hours, missing you," I teased. "Then I might head out into Moscow and do a little retail therapy."

"Will you be rolling around in these sheets naked?"

"Of course."

Oliver shook his head, a smirk playing on his face. "Thanks for the visual," he muttered, leaning down to kiss me goodbye. "I'll leave you to roll around, then."

"Have a good day, Dear," I called, stretching out across the king size bed. Oliver took one glimpse, shook his head at me, and was gone.

I lazed around in bed for the first hour. My activities with Oliver last night had left me quite tired.

Once I was showered and dressed, I decided to explore Moscow. I'd always wanted to visit St. Basil's Cathedral, but never had the chance to go when I'd been on other missions.

I grabbed my phone and purse, noticing I had a message from Georgie. *Oh, shit!* I'd forgotten to call her back.

You better not be ignoring me!

Call me back ASAP!!

Great! She was still angry with me, I could tell by the message. Did I really want to call her right now? I decided to wait until I got into town. At least then I could talk freely.

Moscow was still bitterly cold as I stepped out of the taxi, but Red Square was a hive of activity. There were people everywhere. I saw a coffee shop a few yards away and smiled. Coffee seemed like a good idea to me. It meant I could call Georgie back.

"You took your time!" she spat after the second ring. "I've been going out of my mind with worry! What the fuck are you doing?"

"I'm on a mission, Georgie. You know we can't just drop everything and call each other. I needed to wait until I was alone."

"You're trying to tell me he hasn't left you alone for *two days*?" I held in a giggle. No, actually he hadn't.

"We've been a little busy."

"You do realize how dangerous this is, don't you? Look how leaving him affected you the first time. You're setting yourself up for a huge fall, Jade."

"I'm the only one who could take this mission. Alicia wasn't getting anywhere with it."

"*Alicia* is on this mission, too? Holy shit!" Crap! Why did I just tell her that? "Have you slapped her yet? Oh fuck, did she get it on with Oliver?"

"*No!* He has better taste than that," I snarled. "I've got this, Georgie. Don't worry about me. I want to savor the time I have with him. You know this is all so new to me."

"Who else is going to worry about you, Jelly Bean? You're in love with your target. How the hell are you going to leave him this time?" Telling Georgie the truth was out of the question.

"I'll cross that bridge when I come to it," I whispered, playing with my empty coffee mug.

"I can't watch you fall apart, Jade. Not when I know I can do something about it! I'm going to speak to Sonia!"

She was so interfering! "No! You can't do that! For one, you'll get yourself into trouble!"

"Jade, Seductors aren't supposed to see their targets again. I'd say the rules are void with this mission." Damnit! Georgie always had a way of getting the truth out of me.

"I won't be saying goodbye to him forever."

"What?"

"The Seductors' founder is allowing me to assume the

identity I have right now when my contract is up if I complete this steal." She was silent on the other end of the phone. "Okay, so I'll have to wait four years, but Sonia suggested acting out a kidnapping—something that will be believable."

"Jade, can you hear yourself?" Georgie stressed. "Are you really telling me you can spend the rest of your life *lying* to him? It will eat away at you. You've stolen from him...*twice* by the time this mission is complete!" She'd been spending too much time with Molly, the forecaster of doom.

"Georgie, we can talk about this when we see each other. And please don't tell Molly or Drew. This offer is top secret. They already know too much as it is." I knew I could trust her.

"You know I won't tell anyone, and you're right—we *will* talk about this when I see you!" I couldn't mistake the warning in her voice. She meant business.

"Okay," I sighed as my cell phone chimed, alerting me to a new message. I looked at my phone quickly, seeing a text from Oliver.

Is it wrong that I'm missing you already? xxx

"Is that lover boy texting you?" Georgie asked, teasing.

"Yeah, I need to get back to work. I have a gala to attend tonight."

"Lucky you. Is the sex still amazing?"

"I'm not talking about that over the phone," I sniggered.

"It's that good, huh?" I sighed, thinking back to last night and drowning in the memories of his touch. "I'd be happy for you under different circumstances. You know I would. Just be safe, Jelly Bean."

"I will," I promised just before she hung up. I typed a response to Oliver before putting my phone back away.

It's only been 4 hours. You can't be missing me already. ;) xxx

I was barely out of the coffee shop before his next message came through.

Oh, I'm missing you, Beautiful. Trust me. I can't   wait to see you later. I know I'll find you instantly in the crowd with your beauty. xxx

Mr. Kirkham, you always have such a way with words. xxx

I was smiling to myself as he sent his last message.

Only for you. ;) xxxxxx

He was always the charmer.

✳ ✳ ✳

Alicia didn't want to share the limo with me on the way to the gala. It was written all over her face as she glared at me from across the aisle. Sonia must have told her about taking a few months off the mission. I wasn't going to rise to her bitch brow, though, because truthfully, I didn't give a shit about her.

"Are you going to ignore me the entire way there?" she finally snapped, pulling my gaze away from the window.

"I didn't think we had anything else to talk about," I muttered, looking down at the new purse I'd bought while shopping earlier. It matched my purple dress perfectly.

"You talk about backstabbing...and then you go behind my back to Sonia!" Oh, here we go!

"This mission doesn't need both of us right now. Sonia needs you on other cases," I whispered. We may have been alone, but there was still the driver to think about. "And keep your voice down!" I motioned in the driver's direction. Alicia sat back in her seat and didn't say another word for the rest of the trip.

I knew this gala tonight was a big deal, but I was taken aback by the grandness surrounding me as I entered the main ballroom. Not to mention the room was packed. There had to be at least five hundred people already here. How the hell was I going to find Oliver? Alicia had already stormed off in a different direction than me. I reached the top of the grand staircase, feeling a little like a princess. *You, Jade? A princess?* Okay, it may have sounded stupid, but that's how I felt as I gazed out over the crowd. Holding my head up high, I made my way down the staircase, lifting my dress slightly so I didn't trip on the material.

"Would you allow me to escort you to the bar?" a fair haired man asked as I reached the bottom. I was already scanning the crowd, looking for Oliver. He was here somewhere.

"I'm sorry, I need to find my date," I muttered, not even looking at him.

"He can't be much of a date if he's abandoned you already. Have one drink with me, please." The fair haired guy was just about to touch my arm when a voice came from behind me.

"Miss Gibbs hasn't been abandoned. She is *my* date," Oliver smirked, pulling me against him. The fair haired guy winced awkwardly. Clearly, he knew who Oliver was and scurried off into the crowd. "Jade," he gasped, "you look absolutely breath taking." I wasn't given a chance to respond before he crashed his lips against mine in an aggressive kiss. He tasted so good—of freshness and mint. *Mmm, that was the Oliver taste I knew*. We seemed to forget the world around us. All that mattered were his lips moving against mine.

"Wow," I giggled against his mouth as we broke apart. "That was a kiss hello."

"I want to do so much more, believe me," he muttered in my ear.

"Save that for later," I winked, looking around the crowd, watching all the eyes on us. Oliver and I were causing quite a show, it seemed.

"Are you ready for this?" he grinned, running his hand through my hair. I'd straightened it tonight, going for a simple look to show off my elegant, purple dress more.

"I'm ready," I beamed, taking his hand in mine. He looked down at our joined hands, stroking the side of my palm with his thumb before pulling me deeper into the crowd.

❆ ❆ ❆

"What do you do again, Miss Gibbs?" one of Oliver's male associates asked me later that evening. Oliver was currently on stage, picking some numbers for the drawing tonight.

"Interior design and artwork mainly," I murmured, watching Oliver on stage.

"Interesting. Is that how you and Mr. Kirkham met?" This guy was really nosey and I didn't like it.

"I don't see how that is any of your business," I frowned, watching Oliver step down from the stage and begin to make his way toward me.

"I'm simply making conversation. I've never seen Oliver so happy, that's all." I knew that was true. I could see it deep in his eyes as he got closer to me.

"I'm sorry, I didn't mean to snap like that," I apologized. "It's just that Oliver and I like to keep our relationship private."

"That's understandable," the associate muttered as Oliver wrapped his arms around me from behind.

"Oh, I see you've met Jade, Jeremy," he chuckled, kissing my neck softly.

"You know me, Oliver. I'll always seek out the most beautiful woman in the crowd first."

"Careful, you know she's spoken for," Oliver warned in a teasing tone.

"The most beautiful? I'm not so sure about that." I glanced around the room. The finest on the rich list were all here tonight. I was sure there was even royalty. There was *no way* I could be the most beautiful here.

"You are to me. That's all that matters," Oliver whispered into my ear. "If you'll excuse us, Jeremy," he muttered. "I have more people to introduce Jade to."

"Oh, don't let me keep you. Wonderful to meet you, Jade." Jeremy smiled as Oliver led me away.

"I think I'll have to keep an eye on you all night," he chuckled, guiding me through the crowd as he acknowledged a few faces we passed.

"What do you mean?"

"Jade, you're a vision tonight. You must have noticed all the greedy eyes watching you."

"Umm...no, I can't say that I have," I lied, forcing a blush.

"That's one of the many things I love about you," he grinned, stroking my cheek as he ran his thumb across my bottom lip. *Oh, God! He said the 'L' word again. Breathe, Jade!* "You have no idea how amazing you are."

"And you have a way of rendering me speechless," I giggled, leaning up to peck his desirable lips.

The first part of the evening was spent mingling. All the names and faces over the last few days were giving me a headache, but I managed to commit most of the right names to memory, as well as the information I gathered from them. I'd already managed to eliminate a few scientists from my list by the time Oliver asked me to dance.

"Are you bored yet?" he whispered, pulling me against his chest as we swayed to the beat of the music.

"I'm with you, how could I get bored?" I sighed, running my hands down his chest.

"It won't always be like this. We'll have time to ourselves, too. I just have a lot going on within my company right now."

"Oliver, I don't care. I want you. If this was *all* you did, I'd still take it." His eyes seemed to penetrate my soul as he gazed down at me.

"I've been waiting so long for you to be this open with me. I can hardly believe it."

"This is just the start. I'll open up fully, I promise. Just give me some time." His eyes were soft until he looked out into the crowd of people. "I should have guessed Imogen Windom would turn up," he glared. "That woman can't take a damn hint!"

"Who?" I questioned, turning in the direction that he was glaring.

"Imogen is my rival in every way. She's the CEO of

Windom International. She's been trying to merge our weapons departments for years just so she can take over." Interesting...I could be working for her. Who knew?

"Why would she want to do that?"

"Power. Our companies are the main supplies of nuclear warfare. If we merged, we would be unstoppable. No other company could match us."

"Isn't that what you would want? What's stopping you?"

"Imogen only sees dollar signs. She doesn't care who she sells to." Which meant paying the Seductors to gain a power core would be nothing to her. "That's not how I do business, and why I will *never* merge with her." A photographer from the press suddenly appeared in front of us before I spoke. I buried my face into Oliver's chest. "Jade, what's wrong?"

"I can't have my face in the press," I mumbled into his chest. "Can you ask him to leave, please?" I heard Oliver politely ask the photographer to leave before I lifted my head up to meet his concerned dark eyes. "I'm sorry."

"Are you going to explain what that was all about?"

"I will, but not tonight." I smiled sadly, gripping his shoulders as I pulled myself closer to him. "I don't want to ruin the evening."

"Imogen is here. It couldn't get much worse," he smirked, running his hands down my back. "I'm beginning to see that you have some serious layers, Jade."

"You have no idea," I whispered, resting my head on his chest. I couldn't look him in the eyes...not when I was being so truthful.

"You're lucky. I happen to *love* stripping your layers," he whispered suggestively, running his hands toward my lower back. "If we weren't in a room full of people. I'd start stripping the top layer right now." There went another pair of panties! *Damn you, Mr. Kirkham!*

"How much longer do we need to stay at this party?" I whimpered, holding my legs together. I had no control when it came to sex with this man. He made all the pain disappear with his touch.

"We can leave whenever you want." I could feel his smirk as he spoke.

"Like, right now?"

"We've shown our faces. I can't see my uncle being mad at us if we leave now. I mean, if you were to suddenly have a headache, I'd have to escort you back to the hotel."

"I have an ache, but it's not my head," I whispered into his ear seductively. Okay, that may have been too much for shy Jade, but right then, I just wanted Oliver to take me back to the hotel as fast as he could.

"Jesus, Jade!" he gasped. "You're in *so* much trouble now." Oh good, I loved being in trouble with Oliver. He took my hand, leading me off the dance floor as he pulled his phone out. "Alicia, can you find my uncle and tell him Jade and I are leaving? She isn't feeling too well. I'll see him in the morning at our breakfast meeting." He hung up without a response from her. Oh, she'd love that—a man hanging up on her. I noticed Imogen trying to make her way through the crowd toward us. Oliver spotted her, too. "We need to get out of here before *that* woman catches us."

"Why don't you try the fire exit?" I suggested. He must have thought it was a good idea, because we began to make our way toward it.

"Oliver, are you really going to run out on me without

even saying hello?" Imogen called just before we reached the exit. I watched Oliver compose himself before turning around to face her.

"You know I try to avoid you when I can, Imogen."

"Always the gentlemen, I see," she glared.

"I'm a perfect gentlemen to ladies," he smirked, turning to wink at me. I stood there with my mouth hanging open as I listened to them. They were so openly rude to each other. I'd never seen this side of Oliver before.

"Is that what the blonde is? A lady? I thought she was one of those women that charge by the hour." *What a bitch!*

"Don't make it personal, Imogen," Oliver threatened. "You never won those battles. Jade is more of a lady than you'll *ever* be."

"Jade?" she questioned, tilting her head and looking at me. One sly smile on her face and I was sure this was the bitch I was working for. "Was this the woman you were seen with six months ago?"

"Yes, not that it has anything to do with you," he stressed. "We're leaving. Goodnight, Imogen."

"Lovely to meet you, *Jade*," she grinned as Oliver escorted me away. There was a meaning in her eyes as she said my name, and I feared it was because she might know who I really was. *Fantastic! I might be working for an evil bitch!*

CHAPTER THIRTEEN

"You've been quiet since we left the gala," I muttered, resting my head on Oliver's shoulder as we made our way back to the hotel.

"Imogen does that to me, sorry."

"I thought you were amazing. You stayed so calm."

"She wants a reaction. You should've heard some of the comments she made about my father in the past."

"I'm sorry. You shouldn't have to put up with shit like that."

"Don't worry about me. I can look after myself," he grinned, running his fingertips down my arm.

"I want to look after you, too. That's what I'm here for."

"Is that so?" he mused, his eyes lightening with emotion. "And how are you planning on looking after me?"

"By simply being there for you. I want to do this, Oliver. I want there to be an *us*."

"What happened to taking things slowly?"

"I think you're rubbing off on me," I giggled as the car came to a stop.

"I can think of something I'd like to rub *against* you," he murmured, his voice full of sudden need. A need for *me*.

"Then we better get to the suite quickly, wouldn't you agree?" I grinned, moving to expose my leg as the material slipped off my thigh.

"Fuck, thigh highs? You know what they do to me," he snarled, trying to compose himself.

"I remember your desk in New York *very* well. Why do you think I wore these?" I teased, stepping out of the car after the driver opened the door.

"Get those thigh highs and that sexy body of yours to my suite—now," he threatened, stalking me into the lobby.

My heart was racing as I rushed into the elevator. Luckily, some people got in with us. Oliver's gaze was so predatory, I was sure he'd have made his attack if we'd be alone. He moved behind me, pulling me against him. The suite was on the top floor, so we had a lot of levels to go.

I smiled to myself, feeling his hand graze over my backside. He had about as much control as I did. As I felt his hand creep inside the slit on my dress, I held my breath. Jeez, there were four other people in this elevator. Couldn't he wait a few minutes?

"Mmm…so sexy," he purred into my ear, his fingertips skimming over the top of one of my stockings. I elbowed him playfully in the ribs, trying to move his hand. Shy Jade wouldn't tolerate this kind of behavior. I wondered what he would think if he knew the real me would let me fuck me right here with everyone watching? Would that be too much for him? Was he even the kind of guy who could handle a hellcat like that? *Oh, he could handle the real you and you know it!* But would he *want* to handle the real me? I was snapped out of my thoughts as his hand suddenly slipped inside my panties. Oh, his fingers brushing against my clit felt so good, but before I could start to enjoy the feeling, he removed his hand. *Damn him!* I turned my head to pout, wishing I hadn't as I saw him tasting me, licking his finger clean with his talented tongue. *You fell right into that one, Jade.* I had to admit, *that* was my favorite Oliver trait.

"Oh, God," I whimpered, turning away. A few people glanced back at me, frowning.

"You taste so good," he purred into my ear so only I could hear. "I can't wait to taste it from the source with my tongue." Jesus Christ! How many floors did we have to go? I looked at the panel of lights. *Ten more floors? You have got to be joking!* I could hardly stand. "Would you like that?"

"Yes," I panted a little too loudly, making everyone turn around to look at us. Luckily, most of the people got out at the next stop. There was only one old man left.

Oliver was making slow circles on my back, and it was sending tremors of pleasure all over my body. This was the slowest elevator ride in history. One stop before ours, the old guy got off. The moment the elevator doors closed, Oliver pounced, lifting me up by my ass, crashing his lips against mine.

"Finally," he snarled as the elevator opened on our floor.

With me still in his arms, he walked to our suite, opening the door quickly before attacking my neck with his lips, kissing and nipping.

"Oliver, I'm burning for you," I cried out as his hands began to undo my dress the moment the door closed.

"I'm working on those layers now, Beautiful. Hold on," he cooed, slipping the dress off my body. I stood before him in a white lace bodice and my thigh highs. His eyes looked half crazed as he ran them over my whole body. "Go and lie on my bed right now," he ordered. I frowned. Wasn't he joining me? "I'll be there in a minute. I just need to get something."

"O...kay," I muttered, acting nervous. "Should I be worried?"

"You'll like this, trust me," he winked, darting off into the living area. What was he planning?

I did as he asked and made my way into the bedroom, taking my shoes off before lying on the bed to wait for him.

He came back moments later with his shirt undone and his slacks partly open. I was so distracted by his fine body; I didn't notice what was in his hand at first. An ice bucket? *Oh, ice! Yes, please!*

"I thought we could have a little fun with this," he smirked, placing the bucket on the nightstand before stripping in front of me. All I could do was stare. He was a masterpiece —every single inch of him. "Now, the question is, where do I start?" he mused, stroking his chin. He had slight stubble and I couldn't wait to feel it grazing my thighs.

"I think you should start at the bottom and work your way up," I giggled, stretching my arms out above my head.

"Do you, now?" He moved toward the bottom of the bed like a lion stalking its prey. My heart was beating so fast I could hear it. Oliver finally moved onto the bed, taking my right leg in his hands. Running his fingers all the way to the top, he stopped at my stocking and slowly rolled it down my leg. "As much as I love these, they have to go," he winked, repeating the same process with my left leg.

Once his fingertips had explored every inch of my legs, he lifted me up, unhooked my bodice, and pulled it from my body in one swift movement. Even the way he undressed me made a moisture pool between my legs. He was so gentle and loving, yet I could feel the desire for me ripple through his body as he touched me. "Are you ready for a little ice?" he whispered, his thumbs slowly stroking my hardening nipples.

"Yes," I yearned, arching up to push my breasts further into his hands. He palmed them, gripping roughly for a few short moments before releasing them to collect some ice from the bucket.

He started at my neck, slowly running the ice cube down toward my collarbone. I was already squirming, trying to hold my legs together. The cold trail he left was making every nerve ending in my body feel like a live wire.

"Do you like that?" he whispered, moving the cube lower, gently running it over the top of my breast. My nipples seemed to harden even more just at the thought of ice on them. I nodded my head frantically as he ran it over my right nipple. When he rolled the ice over my hardened skin, making small circles, I hissed at the coldness. "You haven't felt anything yet," he purred, moving to suck my cold nipple into his mouth. I was lost is a blissful, torturous pleasure. The feeling of his warm tongue lapping across my nipple sent sparks right toward my center. I was aching for him.

"Fuck, Oliver," I moaned as he ran the ice over my other nipple, still attacking the first with his mouth. If he continued, I was going to climax and he hadn't even been anywhere near my sex yet.

"Just feel it, Baby. I want you *really* wet—ready for my cock." Once he was satisfied with my nipples, he stretched to get another ice cube. "You've melted the other one," he chuckled.

"It is really hot in here," I panted, fanning myself. I really was burning up.

"It's going to get hotter," he winked, running the ice cube

B. L. WILDE

over my ribcage and then down my stomach. He hooked his fingers into my lace panties, pulling them away from my body.

I was ready to combust. No more ice. I just needed his cock inside me! That was until he began to run the ice along the inside of my thigh. Oliver was right in between my legs, and when he suddenly ran the ice through my slick folds, I gripped the sheets behind me. "Have you ever been fucked with an ice cube before?" *Holy shit! Fucked with an ice cube?*

"N...no!" I groaned, arching off the bed. It was a true statement. I may be a Seductor, but *no one* had ever done this to me before.

"Shit, Jade, I'm not sure the ice cube will last. It's starting to melt already. Are you that hot?"

"You seem to have that effect on me." I watched Oliver remove the ice cube and study it. Oh. My. God! I could read his face before he even did it. He sucked the ice cube into his mouth, and I was done for. He was too damn sexy for words.

"Mmm...delicious," he moaned, moving to get another piece of ice from the bucket. He ran it up and down my clit for a few minutes, my hips rocking against his hands of their own accord. Crap, I was going to cum if he kept going. Being fucked with an ice cube was amazing. The mixture of hot and cold felt *so* good. "Do you want to taste yourself?" I nodded, captivated by him. He brought the ice to my lips and I licked it, tasting myself, which was quite possibly the most erotic thing I'd ever done. "How good do you taste, huh?" he grinned, putting the ice in his mouth. *Greedy bastard.* I nodded with a groan, closing my eyes as I felt his erection push against my overheated sex. "That's enough ice for one night, I think. Are you ready for me, Beautiful?" I didn't need to answer him. Oliver could see it in my eyes, and with one deep thrust, he was inside me. "So damn perfect," he mumbled, moving down to lavish my breasts. His mouth was still cold from the ice and I cried out in pleasure. His cock felt so wonderful sliding in and out of me.

"More, Oliver, I need more!" I pleaded, desperate to reach my brink. I couldn't wait any longer.

"You want it deeper?" he panted.

"YES!" I begged. He lifted my hips at an angle and got onto his knees, pushing right inside me. It. Was. Heaven.

"Like this, Beautiful?" he snarled, thrusting at a maddening pace. "You like it when I really fuck you, huh?"

"F...fuck...yes!" I was losing my mind. All I could feel or see was Oliver, and with one more deep thrust, I came undone, falling into the abyss.

"How was that?" he smirked down at me moments later.

"Can we do that again soon?" I gasped, holding my chest as I tried to catch my breath.

"What makes you think we're finished now?" he smirked, leaning down to capture my lips with his. *God, I loved this man!*

* * *

The plane ride back home was a little uncomfortable. Oliver insisted on me traveling back on his private jet with him, which would have been fine, if Richard *and* Alicia hadn't been on it, too.

The last few days in Moscow flew by and were very informative and fun for me. Oliver spared no expense in spoiling me, taking me to the Opera, the finest restaurants, and the best galleries. I'd never experienced luxury like it. His company and love for me was what made it so special, though.

The factory tour gave me the chance to spend a little more time with Dylan, and watch the bond he and Oliver had. They weren't just employer and employee. I could see that they were friends, too. Dylan and Oliver even confessed to me that Dylan and Macy were trying to develop a new sustainable powercore back in Macon. The issue was with the 'trying.' Did that mean the powercore didn't exist yet? Knowing Oliver the way I did, if the powercore *did* exist, it would have been designed by a scientist he knew and trusted—a friend. I needed better clarification, though. I needed proof.

"You have a meeting in London next week," Richard muttered toward Oliver over his newspaper. "We need to finalize the deal with Steel Manufacturing."

"I wasn't aware we were at that stage already," Oliver frowned, looking over at me sadly. He knew I wouldn't be able to go to London with him. Brian wouldn't let me take more time off. I needed to think of a way to quit my job!

"Alicia and I sealed the deal while you were on the factory tour with Jade," his uncle replied, still refusing to give him any eye contact. You could have cut the tension with a knife.

"And you're only telling me this now? That was almost a day ago."

"You seemed a little distracted after the gala. I thought it was best to wait."

Oliver closed his eyes, clearly trying to calm his temper before speaking. "When do we leave, Alicia?"

"Next Tuesday," she beamed, darting her eyes at me. It didn't make any difference, even with the distance between us. Oliver was still *mine*! "I've added it to your planner and emailed you the contract and notes."

"That was very efficient of you," Oliver thanked. Yeah, that was all Alicia *was* good for—being a PA. "We'll have to make the most of this week back home if I'm going to be away the following week," he mused, turning his attention to me. I nodded, stroking his face gently. "It will only be four days. I can't see it taking longer than that."

"It's fine. You do what you have to do. I'll be in New York waiting for you when you get back." I heard Richard snort as I spoke. Yeah, I had a long way to go until he trusted me again. I was a patient person, though. Deep down, I knew he had reason to dislike me. I was far worse than he could ever imagine.

Eight hours later and I was finally free from Alicia's glares.

"Did you want to come back to my apartment?" Oliver asked, getting into the limo next to me. "I'm sure Mrs. Davis would love to see you." The offer was so tempting, but I needed to send Sonia my progress report. Not to mention, Miles had done a few background checks on the ten possible candidates for the power core.

"I really need to check on my apartment. I still have some boxes to unpack," I sighed. He nodded, dropping his head. "Why don't you stay at my apartment tomorrow night? I'll cook for you."

"Really?" he beamed. Oh, Oliver liked that idea a lot.

"Yes. If I didn't have so much to do, I would stay with you tonight, too. I'm not pulling away, I promise."

"I'm sorry. I'm supposed to be playing this cool and it's not really working, is it?" he chuckled, running his hands through his hair.

"You're playing it just fine," I whispered, leaning in to kiss him deeply. I wrapped my arms around his neck, pulling him to me. By the time we broke apart, he had pinned me against the seat with his body, his erection rubbing against my stomach.

"What is it about us and limos?" he panted, climbing off me while I caught my breath.

"I don't know," I giggled, straightening my top as the limo pulled up to the curb.

"You are just around the corner from me, huh?" he mused, looking up at my apartment building. "Do you need a hand carrying your luggage?"

"I'm fine," I sighed, pecking his lips. "Thank you for a wonderful trip."

"I should be thanking you for coming all the way to Moscow. It's been amazing having you by my side, Jade."

"I'll see you tomorrow night?"

"Nothing would keep me away," he winked, pulling me in for another kiss. This time it was deeper. I had to grip his shoulders for support when our lips parted.

Stepping out of the limo, I turned back to him as Duncan grabbed my bags. "I can help you with your bags if you want, Miss Gibbs."

"I'm fine, thank you, Duncan," I smiled. "Bye, Oliver."

"Bye, Beautiful," he beamed. "Oh, I'll need your apartment number."

"24A," I called. "Anytime after seven is fine. I'll be home."

"I can't wait." He winked suggestively before finally closing the door. He had a point; I couldn't wait, either.

✻ ✻ ✻

"I take it you were with Oliver while you were off?" Brian commented while we worked on finalizing the design plans.

"I don't see how that is any of your business," I muttered, looking down at my drawings. I hated having to play shy Jade around this asshole.

"You took a week off when we're in the middle of an important project! Had I known it was to follow Oliver Kirkham around, I wouldn't have authorized it!"

"I'm freelance. I can do whatever I want!"

"I worry about my employees, Jade. Oliver Kirkham is a playboy. I'm just trying to look out for you." *Playboy?* He didn't know Oliver at all.

"Oliver makes me happy. That's all I care about."

Brian stretched his hand out, stroking my arm. "I could make you happier." I pulled back, glaring at him. Would this guy ever take the hint? I wasn't interested!

"I don't like your advances toward me, Brian."

"There's a connection between us. Don't try to deny it," he stated, moving closer toward me, trapping me against the wall. There was going to be a *connection* alright if he tried to touch me! I needed to quit this damn job right now! I'd had enough of this slimeball! "You don't need Oliver Kirkham when you can have me." Was he for real? "Don't settle for him. He's only focused on his career, so you'll get lost in his world. He'll forget you like all the other women before. Stop fighting it, Jade. You know we would be so good together." Before his hand even touched my face, I pushed him sharply, twisting his arm behind his back. He yelled out in pain. Brian was lucky; I wanted to do far worse.

"I've had enough of your disgusting advances toward me. I quit," I seethed, into his ear.

"Ah, J…Jade, please! Let's talk about this," he panted. I pulled his arms tighter, knowing it was almost at the breaking point. Drew had taught me this hold years ago. "Ow, fuck! Okay, okay. I get it! I accept your resignation."

"Thank you," I grinned, letting him go. I collected my bag and coat, ready to leave. When I turned back around, Brian was standing back up.

"Are you sure you're not running because of your sexual urges for me?" he called before I made it through the door. Oh, now he'd overstepped the mark. I was done playing nice!

"Sexual urges?" I questioned, making him think he stood a chance with me as I stalked back toward him.

"I could drive you crazy, Baby. All you have to do is say the word. I've wanted you since the moment you came for an interview. You could have been a dumb blonde and I'd have still given you the job. Stop fighting it. Let me fuck you right here, right now." I gave him a shy smile, dropping my bag and coat as I stalked toward him. "I fucking knew it. That's it, bring that sexy ass of yours to me," he ordered with a grunt. I needed to get as close as possible to this asshole for what I had planned. The moment I wrapped my arms around his neck, his hands were on my ass. "I'm going to fuck you on my desk! I've been dreaming about doing that for weeks."

"That sounds wonderful," I purred, stroking his jawline. His lips parted at my simple touch. "But there is one problem with that."

"Which is?" he asked, looking down at me in confusion. I slammed my knee hard into his groin at his words, releasing my arms from around his neck so he fell to the floor.

"That I don't find you attractive in the slightest, you

asshole!" I snarled, grabbing my coat and bag again. Oh, the satisfaction of watching him roll around on the floor in agony.

"J...J...Jade, don't tell Oliver about this, please!" Brian called from the floor. "He'll skin me alive."

"You should have thought about that before you made a pass at me. Goodbye, Brian. I won't be needing a reference from a slimeball like you." With that, I left, slamming his door behind me.

Thank fuck that job was over.

I knew Oliver was in meetings all day, and I didn't want to worry him while he was at work. He'd be showing up at my apartment in four hours anyway. He wasn't going to take the news about Brian well, but at least he'd be happy that I quit.

Alicia would be taking some time off work due to a sudden illness hopefully in the next week. It might even work to my advantage. Oliver would need a replacement as soon as possible. I could offer my services until he found someone.

❈ ❈ ❈

I was cooking Mexican food tonight. Oliver wanted to see some of my layers, and that was what I was planning to do. It was time to allow him to see parts of the real Jade, and her favorite food was Mexican.

I was preparing dinner when I got a call from Miles. He must have finished the searches I'd asked for.

"Hey," I answered, holding the phone on my shoulder with the side of my face while I continued to get the prep done for tonight.

"Hi, Jade. Is now a good time to talk?"

"Sure, I'm alone."

"Okay, so I've been able to eliminate a few other scientists from your list. I'm sending you all the information as we speak, but you only have three possible names now."

"Three? Miles, how the hell did you manage that?"

"I looked into their expenditures. If you're dealing with advances in nuclear weapons, you're going to need space for testing at some point. Whether it be atmospheric, exoatmospheric, underground, or underwater, that all takes money, and a lot of it." *Exoatmospheric...what?* Miles was such a nerd.

"But what if this core doesn't even exist yet?"

"They'd still need the space to test, Jade. Why else would they have made the machine? Do you want to know the three names that Kirkham Industries has bought or funded space for?"

"Yes," I muttered, mixing the sauce I was making.

"Dr. Dylan Reynolds is the first." I wasn't at all surprised to hear his name. "His space is underground. Kirkham Industries has owned it for over forty years, but I can't pinpoint a location yet. Dr. Carlton has a space in Russia, which seemed odd to me, but maybe the land was cheaper. It was acquired five years ago, and Kirkham Industries only funded some of the money. The last name, Dr. Fellows, is linked closely to N.A.T.O. His space in Arizona was purchased by Kirkham Industries over thirty years ago."

"And you think they are the only scientists capable of making this powercore?"

"They all check out, Jade. They're well known fusion experts and all have the equipment necessary to develop the powercore. I can't see how any of the other people on the list could achieve it when they don't have the resources."

"Why are you so damn smart?" I teased. Miles was a genius.

"If you find this powercore, you do realize the impact it's going to have, right?"

"What do you mean?"

"I was looking at the blueprints you stole months ago. The amount of mass these machines have. You're looking at a reaction three times larger than any nuclear weapon ever produced. Jade, if this core is real, whoever owns it owns the entire world." *Holy shit!*

"Why are you telling me this?"

"If you can't find the powercore, our client wants Oliver Kirkham kidnapped and tortured until he confesses." *No!* Oliver being tortured? I couldn't stop the tears stinging my eyes. I wouldn't let that happen. "Jade, this mission is unlike anything we've ever done before. You need to make sure you are completely focused. Everything is riding on this."

"When did The Seductors become so greedy?"

"It's evolution. Diamond necklaces and files aren't enough for them anymore. They want more power, and with a steal like this, higher paying clients will take notice. The Seductors are becoming the undisputed leaders in our field."

"You're making it sound like we're turning into the Secret Service," I snorted, trying to keep the conversation light, when really, I was still reeling about Oliver's fate if I didn't find the powercore.

"That wouldn't be too far from the truth. We could easily match them."

"Is that everything?"

"Alicia is being called back to headquarters next Friday. I've already started the paperwork on her medical records."

"Make the illness as nasty as you can," I teased.

"Jade, I can't give her a *real* illness," he chuckled.

"Shame," I muttered, smirking to myself.

"If I find any more information, I'll send it over to you."

"I only have three names to check. I don't think you could do much more," I giggled.

"You know what I mean, and Jade, please be careful."

"I always am. Thanks, Miles," I sighed before we both hung up.

I wasn't surprised to hear his views on where he thought the Seductors were heading. I'd noticed how our clientele had changed over the last few years, and had sensed a movement toward the higher paying clients. It relieved me to know I had less than five years remaining on my contract. Who knew where they would be by that time. I was sure it wouldn't be the same organization. Sonia had been hoping I would stay on after my contract ended. It wasn't uncommon for some top Seductors to stay on and coach new recruits to help hone their skills. Sarah, the Seductor who found me in Indianapolis, had done just that. She still came to headquarters from time to time with her words of wisdom, but most of her involvement was done *behind* the scenes. Before Oliver, I would have jumped at the chance to stay on. Now I was counting down the time I had left.

Of course, I had the mission to complete first. Now that I knew Oliver would be kidnapped and tortured if I didn't find the powercore, I had no choice. I *needed* to find it. I had to keep him safe.

CHAPTER FOURTEEN

I had just finished getting ready when a knock came at my door. Oliver was always so punctual. After quickly ensuring that the table was all set for dinner, I took in my appearance in the mirror. I'd never looked more like the real Jade around him before, and wondered what he'd think of me in my tiny denim shorts and favorite black Guns and Roses T-shirt. I was a little nervous at seeing his reaction.

"Are you ever late for anything?" I giggled, opening the door to him. He was wearing faded jeans and a crisp black shirt. Christ, maybe I should skip dinner and take him right to bed.

"I'm never late for the important things," he grinned as I widened the door so he could come in. I noticed he had an overnight bag in his hand.

"I see you came prepared," I mused, motioning toward his bag. "Are you planning on leaving your toothbrush here for future visits?"

"Only if you do the same at my apartment," he smirked, his eyes raking me in as he dropped his bag. "Guns and Roses, huh? I should have guessed."

"You said you wanted to see some of my layers," I pointed out. "This is one. I'm a total rock chick. This is my casual attire."

A playful look crossed his face before he pulled me into his arms. "I like your casual look," he murmured, crashing his lips against mine, gripping my ass roughly. "My favorite look on you is naked, though, but we can wait until after dinner if that's what you want." He expected me to decide if we had sex right now or not? *Jade, you've just spent three hours in the kitchen. You can wait an hour. Control yourself.*

"I don't want to wait…" Oliver's hands began to creep into my top. "But I've spent hours making dinner for you." He stopped his attack, pulling back to gaze into my eyes.

"Let's eat then. It smells amazing," he beamed, pecking my lips. "This is a nice place."

"It's smaller than I would have liked, but New York prices are crazy."

"You're not wrong there," he mused, still looking around.

The apartment wouldn't have been my first choice, but it was close to Oliver; that was all that mattered. It was an open plan with a light paint on the walls giving it a little color. The kitchen was compact, but that was all I needed. The single bedroom didn't have the same effect as the apartment I'd been staying at in St. Petersburg, but it had a larger bed. What more did I need?

"The bedroom is the first door on the right."

"And you're telling me that because you want dinner *first*?" he teased, looking back at me. He could be such a cocky asshole sometimes.

"I wasn't sure if you wanted to put your bag in there or not, actually," I countered with my hands on my hips. "I have some restraint."

"You do?" he gasped, acting shocked. Okay, it was a lie, but we *were* going to eat first. I was making that my main mission tonight. *No, Jade, you're a Seductor. Your mission is to find that powercore.* "Well, I don't."

"Yes, I'm aware of that," I giggled, turning to check on the enchiladas in the oven.

"I brought some wine. I wasn't sure what you were cooking, so I have red and white," he said, holding up two bottles.

"That was very thoughtful. I decided on Mexican food tonight, and made chicken enchiladas for us."

"From scratch?" Oliver sounded impressed. I nodded, looking away shyly. "Is this you shedding some of your layers?" he whispered, wrapping his arms around me from behind.

"Yes," I panted, feeling his lips brush against my neck. "I want you to know me. The *real* me."

"I can see that now, Beautiful." He sucked on my earlobe. "Just keep peeling those layers in your own time, though. I don't want to put any pressure on you." Forget the layers, I wanted to peel out of my damn clothes right now!

"Dinner *is* going to be ruined," I said breathlessly, gripping the counter as his fingertips began to play with the button on my shorts. "Why don't you pour us a glass of wine?"

"That's not going to keep me busy for long," he mused, running his hand up my backside. "These shorts are driving me crazy. Do you have any idea how sexy your ass looks in them?"

"Do you *want* this meal to be ruined?" I giggled. He smirked at me, moving away to pour the drinks.

Dinner was pretty tasty, in my opinion. Oliver cleared his plate, which was a good sign, too.

"What did you think?" I asked, getting up to take his plate.

"Your talents are endless. I've yet to find a fault in you, Beautiful." I was glad I had my back to him so he couldn't see my face. Faults—I was full of them. "Why don't you leave the cleaning up until later?" he called, making me turn to look at him.

"I'm only loading the dishwasher. It won't take long. I need to tell you something anyway, but you have to promise me you won't get mad."

"Why would I get mad?" he frowned, standing up and walking toward me.

"I quit my job today," I whispered, not meeting his gaze.

"You think I'd be *mad* about that? Jade, that's the best news I've had all day," he snorted, pulling me into his arms and tilting my chin so I had to look up at him. "Oh…there's more, isn't there?" he mused, concerned. "What happened, Sweetheart?"

"You were right about him," I mumbled, clutching at his shirt. "He…he made a pass at me."

"WHAT?!" Oh, crap! Oliver was pissed.

"Please, can we just forget it? I've already quit, and before I left, I told him he was a slimeball. It's over."

"Why didn't you call me? Did he hurt you?" he soothed, stroking my face. "I'll be paying him a visit! The fucking asshole!"

"NO! Please, Oliver! He didn't even touch me. I kneed him in the balls before he even got close."

"You did?" he smirked, looking at me in awe.

"Yes. There is only one man whose touch I crave," I purred, playing with the buttons on his shirt, distracting him from his rage. He didn't need to save me from Brian. He had already been dealt with.

"Is that so?" he mused, cupping my butt and pulling me flush against his semi-hard erection. "Are you done cleaning up?"

"Yes," I gasped. "The rest can wait."

"Eager, are we?"

"I always am for you." I smiled shyly, taking his hand, pulling him toward my bedroom. My body was already on fire in anticipation. "Can I try leading this time?" I asked, feeling his lips skim my neck as we stood in my bedroom. "I want to savor you."

"Why?" he gasped, moving to look at me with his blazing, dark eyes.

"Because you mean so much to me. I want to show you."

"How can I resist that plea?" he beamed; his eyes alive with emotion. *Don't get carried away, Jade. This isn't an invitation to fuck him senseless.*

I gave him a small smile, unbuttoning his shirt. "For once, you're going to be naked before me." Oliver nodded, trying to hide his amusement. "You really do have an incredible body," I mused, running my nails down his chest once his shirt had fallen to the floor.

"Right back at you, Beautiful," he breathed, running his fingertips down my neck to the top of my breasts.

"Don't distract me," I giggled, slapping his hand away.

"What are you planning on doing to me exactly?"

I gave him a playful grin before speaking. "I want to kiss every inch of your amazing body," I smoldered, undoing the button on his jeans and slowly pulling his zipper down. His erection was already straining in his boxers. "Umm…I think you like that idea, too," I purred, cupping him.

"Jesus, Jade. I never had you down as a tease," he groaned, throwing his head back. *Oh, you have no idea, Oliver!*

I pushed him down onto my bed, hooking my fingers into

his boxers. His cock sprang free as I pulled them down, and I licked my lips when I gazed up at him. I never was a girl who could leave the best part until last. I took one long lick along the side of his cock from base to tip, his grunts and groans calling right to my overheated sex. I began to work him with my mouth, playing with his balls while swirling my tongue around him over and over again. Sucking his tip, I gazed up at him with my hooded eyes.

"Fuck! J...Jade...I'm...I'm..." He didn't get a chance to finish before he came hard and hot down the back of my throat. *Yep, that's how fast I can make you cum!*

I began to strip down to my underwear, watching him catch his breath. I was stepping out of my shorts when he looked up, paralyzing me with his hungry gaze.

"Bring that sexy mouth of yours to me right now!" he ordered. I gave in with a giggle, crawling up his body. "How many glasses of wine have you had tonight?" he questioned, my lips grazing his jaw.

"Two and a half. Why?" I frowned, freezing against his mouth. Had I gone too far?

"I'm trying to work out if this is the wine or you opening up to me more," he murmured, running his hand through my hair.

"I think it's a bit of both," I admitted, pulling on his bottom lip. He responded with a groan, rolling so I was underneath him.

"Now it's my turn." He dipped his hand inside my panties, running his fingers into my slick folds. "Oh, baby! Between your hot mouth and this..." He rubbed my clit slowly. "I can hardly control myself. I want to be everywhere at once. I want to consume your every breath."

"Take me, Oliver. Just take me," I pleaded, lifting my hips up as he continued a slow and tortuous pace with his fingers.

"I could get used to feeling your hot mouth around my cock, Beautiful," he murmured, pulling my bra cups down before sucking my left nipple into his mouth. "You have so many talents," he mused, leaning up to capture my lips with his. I moaned as he inserted two fingers inside me. I was so wet that his fingers slipped in with ease.

"I could say the same about you," I groaned against his lips.

"Is that a request for my mouth to go exploring?" He moved down my neck again. Oh, God! Was he asking if I wanted him to go down on me? "Tell me what you want, Beautiful."

"I want your mouth on me."

"It already is," he chuckled into the swell of my breasts.

"Ugh…lower!" I panted, feeling his fingers twist, hitting that special spot inside me.

"Lower like this?" he purred, nipping along my stomach. I arched my back, feeling myself begin to build. Did he want me to beg?

"Ugh…lower. LOWER!" I moaned before he finally moved between my legs, taking a slow lick across my clit.

"Is this what you wanted, Baby?" he murmured into my heat, licking and sucking my bundle of nerves. I was on the verge of exploding around him.

"Y…yesssssss," I moaned, fisting the sheets as my orgasm hit me. Oliver kissed his way back up my body while I regained my equilibrium.

"I missed you last night," he whispered once we were face to face. "I'm already finding it hard to sleep without you next to me." I gave him a lazy grin, stroking his face lovingly. "Too much information?"

"No," I giggled, rolling to straddle him. "But I'm still too horny to talk right now." A playful look crossed his face, and within seconds, he'd ripped my panties clean off my body and thrust deep inside me. I leaned back, holding his knees while he lifted my hips up and down, slamming into me over and over again. Would I ever tire of his love making?

* * *

"What are you going to do for an income now that you've quit your job with Brian?" Oliver asked hours later when I was wrapped up in his arms.

"I'm not sure. I'll find something," I yawned.

"You could finish designing my office if you needed something right away. What's your rent on this place? Do you need me to cover it for you?"

"Oliver," I sighed, looking up at him. He was too sweet for words, but I didn't want his money. "I have money put aside. I'll be alright. Don't worry about me."

"I can't help but worry. I want you to be happy, Jade." The sincere tone in his voice made my heart leap.

"I *am* happy," I beamed, pecking his lips. "Although, finishing the redesign of your office isn't a bad idea. It will keep me busy."

"Oh, I have several ways to keep you busy." He captured my lips once more, and I gave in with a giggle.

* * *

"Are you sure you don't want to come to London with me?" Oliver muttered over the phone. As tempting as it was, I couldn't. I'd been called back to headquarters for a debriefing while he was away.

"If I wasn't visiting Drew and Georgie in Macon, you know I would," I sighed. "I'm sorry."

"It's not your fault," he breathed, frustrated. "Alicia leaving suddenly like that has left my office a little chaotic."

"Any news when she'll be back?"

"No, and I have no idea if I should get a temp in or just replace her. I can't leave it too long. My receptionist is trying hard enough to cope, but she has her own duties."

"Look, I know this might be a crazy idea, but I'm out of work right now. I can help you if you want. I've done PA work in the past."

"You'd do that for me?" His voice was full of wonder.

"Think about it while you're in London. I know you don't like to mix business with pleasure, but it would only be temporary. We can discuss it when you get back."

"At my place or yours?" I had yet to visit Oliver's apartment. Since our Mexican evening last week, he had practically lived at mine. It was our solace away from prying eyes.

"Yours, if you want," I suggested. "Is Mrs. Davis going to scold me, too?" I teased.

"She'd never do that. She's happy you're back in my life." *Oh.* "You'd really come and work for me?"

"Until you know what is happening with Alicia—yes."

"What did I ever do to deserve you?"

"Call me when you land. I'll already be in Macon by then."

"Okay, Beautiful. I'll see you in a few days. Bye."

"Bye," I breathed as we both hung up. Looking at the time, I realized I needed to get a move on if I was going to catch my flight.

* * *

"Are you avoiding my questions?" Georgie glared as we sat waiting for Miles in the main conference room.

"I can't tell you anything. You *know* that!" I snapped. "If you carry on like this, I'm going to sit by Jack," I threatened. Jack was the loner Seductor who always kept to himself.

"I'm worried about you. You're lucky Drew is on a mission. He wants to beat your ass, too, for taking this assignment."

"I had no choice. Sonia wanted me on it. Please, can we just leave it!?" I snapped as Miles entered the room.

"Hi, everyone. Okay, so I have new tracker software today and some of you aren't going to be too happy about it." Oh, God, I knew what this was. The human chipping devices had been approved. "This is for your own safety," he continued. "And you knew it was coming. You're all being chipped today."

"We aren't fucking animals, Miles," Georgie snapped. "This is fucking ridiculous."

"You have no say. It's come straight from the top. The trackers on your phones aren't enough anymore—especially after what almost happened to Faith." What had almost happened? "Jade, you're up first," Miles called, snapping me from my thoughts. *Great!*

It didn't hurt getting chipped, which I hadn't expected. It was so small I hardly felt it as he injected it just under my hairline on the back of my neck.

"So this means we can't hide anywhere?" I mused while he checked my signal.

"We just want to look after our assets. It will keep you all safe." *Assets?* That's what we were now?

"Really? To me it seems like just another way of keeping tabs on us," Georgie snapped, glaring at Miles with her hands on her hips.

"You know the rules, G," Miles smiled sadly. "You all signed up for this. It's one of the *rules*." The *rules* that most of us had broken from time to time. I tried not to laugh.

✵ ✵ ✵

"What was all that about Faith?" I asked Georgie later on by the pool.

"Her mission went Code One." Oh no! Code One meant a Mission had been compromised, and a clean up team would be implemented to complete the mission. It meant her target might have been killed, too.

That sent shivers down my spine, making me think about *my* target—the man I loved with every ounce of my soul. Clean up would have to kill me first before they got anywhere near Oliver.

"What happened? Do we know?"

"The gossip is that her target worked out what she was doing. She was beaten within an inch of her life. Clean up was searching for her for four days." Now the trackers made sense.

"Poor Faith," I muttered. I'd only spoken to her a few times in the last year, but she seemed like one of the nicer Seductors here.

"Yeah, this is why you need to be careful. What if you have the same fate?"

"Oliver would never beat me within an inch of my life," I chuckled, shaking my head at her. "Stop being so dramatic."

"Jade, everyone knows this is *the* top mission. You're in over your head and you know it!"

"I can complete this assignment!"

"I wasn't talking about the mission. I'm talking about your feelings. Do you really think you're going to be allowed to keep him if you complete the steal?"

"I'm signing the paperwork later today, when Sonia gets back."

"You can willingly lie to him for the rest of your life?"

"Georgie, if that's what I have to do to keep him, then yes."

"You can't keep doing this."

"Doing what?" I fumed, annoyed. Couldn't she just be happy for me?

"Running. You need to accept that Mina's death was a tragic accident. You can't keep blaming yourself."

"Don't bring her into this!" I yelled, my chest aching as my past began to stab at my heart one beat at a time. Georgie knew nothing. It was *all* my fault!

"Jade, you need closure on this. It's been what—almost ten years?" Unable to take anymore of her shit, I stood up, knocking my chair over before storming away, ignoring Georgie's calls. Closure for Mina—I'd never get that. I *was* the only reason she died.

Georgie was right about one thing, though. What was I doing pulling Oliver into all of this? I needed to find the strength to let him go, but I was in too deep. I couldn't just walk away

* * *

"Does the contract meet your approval?" Sonia asked while I was rereading it. There were no clauses, and the contract was definitely binding—even the founder had initiated it. "As you can see, the only way this contract can become void is if Mr. Kirkham discovers who you really are or learns about The Seductors."

"And it's as easy as that? Once my contract is up you'll let me go to him?"

"Yes. I think the kidnap approach is the best way to seal this deal. It will give you the strongest alibi for your four years of absence. We could even use it to our advantage when we secure this powercore. Miles tells me you are extremely close. Our client is very impressed with you, Jade." Why did the vile Imogen Windom come to mind? "I knew you could do this."

"Before I sign this, I want to make one thing clear." I squared my shoulders, ready to make Sonia understand just what I'd do to keep Oliver safe. "If this powercore doesn't exist, or for some unexpected reason I fail this mission, clean up will have to go through me to get to Oliver. Do you understand?"

"*Jade*!" Sonia gasped. "You don't know what you're saying. You'll be killed!"

"If you kill him, I'm as good as dead anyway."

"Jade, think about this. He is *just* a man!" No, he wasn't. He was the life I never thought I deserved.

"I *will* do everything in my power to complete this mission, don't get me wrong, but for once, it's *not* for the

Seductors. I'm doing this to keep Oliver safe. That's all I care about." He wouldn't be tortured. Clean up wouldn't get their hands on him.

"Complete this mission and he *will* be safe," Sonia glared, her tone guarded. I nodded, looking down at that contract again before finally signing it.

"I never thought you'd be this gullible, falling for a rich man. Is it his wealth that attracts you so much?" I was offended.

"It has *nothing* to do with his money, Sonia. Oliver makes me feel alive. He makes me feel…better about myself," I admitted. "He makes me forget my past and what I've done."

"Well, complete this mission, finish your contracted years, and you can have him," she stated, taking the contract. "I'll keep it in your file. I'll also email you a copy for your reference."

"Thank you."

"How close are you to finding the powercore?"

"I'll be working for him by next week. I already have my suspicions with regards to the scientists. If this core exists, he'll tell me. It's only a matter of time."

"Go. Make your preparations. I want a status update weekly. Our client is very keen to know about your progress." I nodded before getting up and leaving.

❋ ❋ ❋

"Please tell me you're coming out tonight?" Georgie pouted, giving me her puppy dog eyes.

"I was thinking of flying back to New York tonight. Oliver gets back tomorrow evening."

"But it's Eve's farewell party. We're only going into town

for a few drinks." It was never a *few* drinks when Seductors went out partying together.

"I'll come out for a few. Then I'm catching my flight home."

"*Home*?" Georgie gasped. "Jeez, you *do* have it bad." I didn't give a crap. Oliver *was* my home.

※ ※ ※

I sat at the table watching Eve, Georgie, Kara, and Daisy dance on the bar. Men were trying to put money in their pants as a joke. That was the problem when a few Seductors went out together; we drew a lot of attention. Eve was British, and I loved her dry sense of humor. There were a few different nationalities in the Seductors, allowing some diversity. Our company was all about gaining the right talents and knowledge, and that meant searching far and wide.

"Aren't you drinking tonight, Jade?" Ryan shouted in my ear, coming up behind me. Ryan was Irish, and one of the six clean up crew leaders. He was a stocky, dark haired guy. The members of the clean up crew were the deadliest of the Seductors. They were the only ones who had the power and tools to kill and destroy. Ryan and Eve had been close over the last few years, and it made me wonder what he was going to do now that she was leaving.

"No, I have a flight to catch later," I smiled, looking back at Georgie who was giving some random guy a lap dance. She was a nightmare!

"I don't know how Eve is going to cope without all this," Ryan mused, smiling at them all dancing on the bar.

"Wasn't she offered the chance to stay?" I questioned. Ryan shook his head. Eve must not have been a high enough earner to be allowed that opportunity. "I'm sure she'll do fine." I grinned, looking back at Eve, feeling envious. Why couldn't it be *my* contract that was up?

* * *

"You're leaving already?" Georgie pouted, hugging me a while later.

"I've had a few drinks," I pointed out.

"Okay. I'll miss you, Jelly Bean. Please be careful." I rolled my eyes, hugging her back. "I think I might sleep with Evan tonight. Have you seen those abs?"

"You be careful, too," I warned. He was part of the clean up crew, but seemed like an okay guy.

"I always am," she protested. Now, I knew that wasn't true. I said my goodbyes to Eve, wishing her luck for the future, before heading back to headquarters to collect my luggage.

Miles was still up when I got back. I saw his office light on.

"Don't you ever have fun, Miles?" I called, startling him as I peered around his door. "You should have come for a drink tonight. You could have let your team handle everything for a few hours."

"I'm too busy keeping all of you safe," he smiled, frowning at his computer screen.

"Is everything okay?" I asked, concerned.

"It's nothing that I can't handle," he sighed. "How is everything going with Mr. Kirkham? Did you get all the information I sent over?"

"Yes, thank you. I'll hopefully start working for him next week, and I can look into the scientists more closely then."

"Good," he muttered, still looking at his screen. He never had been much of a talker.

"Well, I'm about to catch my flight back to New York now." He didn't even look up at me.

"Jade," he called as I was about to leave. I turned back to look at him. "Don't be reckless on this mission. Think about yourself, too."

"Sonia told you, didn't she?" I mused.

"You'd really risk your life for this target, when he doesn't even know who you really are?"

"Yes," I confessed, watching the surprise cross Miles face.

"You're stealing a weapon that is going to change the way we look at war, and you think you'll be able to be with him and not be affected by that?"

"I can't do this any other way. I need to be with him. This client is after the powercore and machine, do you know who they are?" I knew he did but couldn't tell me.

"Stop fishing, Jade."

"Isn't the founder even slightly concerned about who will end up with these machines?"

"Nuclear warfare is a delicate subject. They keep the peace more than start a war. It's all about control."

"But this machine is different, you said so yourself. Whoever has this machine, rules. Surely The organization is taking it too far?"

"They accepted this mission with the understanding that NATO would replace all the nuclear weapons with this new machine. They don't think anything will change. We'll just have more powerful nuclear weapons to keep the peace with."

"You're thinking our client might sell outside of NATO?" I gasped. It had to be Imogen Windom. Oliver had already told me she didn't care who she did business with.

"That's the problem, Jade. I can't be sure, but if they do go rogue, we might have World War III on our hands." *Breathe, Jade!* "Do you see now? This isn't just about you and your target. You can't be reckless! Don't let your heart rule this mission. There is too much at stake."

"Okay, I get it. I'll be careful," I sighed. "But you need to promise me something." He frowned at me. "If you discover these weapons *are* going to be sold outside of NATO, you need to tell me. We can't let that happen, Miles. This is bigger than any of us. If we can stop a war from breaking out, we have to —no matter the cost." He nodded sadly. This was getting too serious. Why did it feel like I had the weight of the world on my shoulders? It suddenly dawned on me that this was what Oliver had to deal with every day, and my heart ached for him.

CHAPTER FIFTEEN

"Did you really threaten Brian?" I gasped with my hand over my mouth. "Oliver, he's your friend!"

"I simply warned him off you when I bumped into him at the airport. And he lost my friendship the moment he made a play for you."

"I told you I had already handled it."

"I know, but I was angry. Brian has always thought he was the big man. I put him back in his place."

"Can we get back to my job offer, please?" I sighed, secretly happy that Oliver had spoken to that slimeball. I'd never had a guy go all alpha male on me before, and I had to admit, I liked it.

"Are you sure about this?" he mused, staring at me from across the table. He was wining and dining me in style tonight at a five star restaurant. You would have thought we'd been apart for weeks rather than days.

"I wouldn't have offered if I wasn't," I grinned, sipping my wine. "If you think it's unprofessional, I completely understand, but it would only be temporary. I just want to help you."

"Okay," he grinned.

"Okay? As in yes? Or no, it's unprofessional?" I questioned.

"Yes," he breathed, taking my hand in his across the table. "Although, I'm not sure how much work we'll get done. You're very distracting."

"We'll set some boundaries."

"I don't like the sound of that," he pouted. *Jeez, those lips!*

"Only for work," I giggled. "I think it's necessary, seeing as you're kind of my boss now."

"Mmm…why does that thought turn me on so much?" he purred, looking at his watch. "It's late. Let's go back to my apartment. We can discuss the rest in bed." *I loved his bossy side!*

"How can I refuse an offer like that?" I beamed, letting him escort me out of the dining room.

Oliver's apartment hadn't changed at all. It was still just as huge and luxurious as the first time I'd been there.

"Does this feel strange for you, too?" he asked, taking off his jacket and tie.

I nodded. "A lot has happened since I was here last," I sighed, running my fingertips across his grand, dining room table, noticing his name that he'd scratched into it when he was a child. "I remember you telling me about this," I smiled.

"Yeah, I'd never seen my father so mad," he chuckled, shaking his head as he got lot in his thoughts.

"How is your father?" I wasn't sure if I'd gone too far judging by his reaction. "I'm sorry. Look, we can talk about something else," I rebuffed, touching his arm.

"No, it's fine. It's just…we had to move him from the family home four months ago. He isn't dealing well with the facility he's in. It confuses him." Oliver had to deal with all this *and* my disappearance. I was a monster.

"You had all this to deal with *four months* ago?" I whimpered, fighting the tears stinging my eyes.

"Hey, don't," he soothed, pulling me into his arms. "I know what you're thinking, and we're past that now. We were both to blame. I rushed you, and it was wrong of me. Okay, you should have been honest too, but we're here now. I know you're not going anywhere. I trust you." Oh, God, this was so painful. What the hell was I doing?

"You do?" I whispered, playing with the collar of his shirt.

"You're different this time." His hand swept my hair behind my shoulder and then stroked my neck and chin. "More open. That's all I've ever wanted." I closed my eyes, crashing my lips against his to hide my tears. We'd done enough talking tonight. He responded, groaning into my mouth before picking me up by my ass, carrying me up his grand staircase.

When he set me down on my feet, I gazed around his bedroom. It hadn't changed at all.

"I've been mostly rough with you since we got back together," he whispered, slowly pulled my jacket off my shoulders. "But I want to take my time tonight. I'm going to cherish you. Would you like that?"

"Yes." My voice came out as a gasp. His fingers gently peeled me out of my dress. Would I ever become accustomed to his touch?

"I'll never get enough of this." He trailed his fingers down my back, stopping at the elastic on my panties. "Do you have any idea what you do to me?"

"I have an idea," I moaned, feeling his hands slip into my panties from behind. Oliver ran his hands between my butt before finding what he was searching for.

"Oh, Jade. What makes you so wet? Is it the anticipation? You know what I'm capable of doing, and that excites you, doesn't it?" How did he know that? "I can make you wetter," he murmured, running his fingers through my slick folds. "You know I can. The question is...do I keep using my fingers or do I change to my tongue?" I held in a whimper. Both were pretty damn good choices. I didn't really care, but there was something about having his head in between my legs that drove me just that little bit more crazy. "You know what I prefer," he smirked, moving to sit on the bed and then pulling me so I was standing in front of him. *Oh no!* Please don't tell me he was going to make me stand up for this. Gently, he pulled my panties down my legs.

"Step," he ordered when they hit the floor. I did as I was told, grabbing his shoulders for support as he slowly trailed his hands up my legs. Oliver slipped his fingers back inside me, caressing my inner walls. My nails dug into his back while I fought to stand up straight. "I could watch you all day and night when you're like this, Beautiful. Under my spell—you mesmerize me." More wetness gushed in between my legs. "And I thought it was just my dirty mouth that turned you on," he mused, noticing my arousal. Leaning in to kiss my belly button, he gazed up at me with hooded eyes. *He was so goddamn perfect!*

"Everything about you turns me on."

"Is that so?" He spoke into my stomach, his lips brushing against my skin while his fingers continued their slow, torturous pace inside me. He was driving me crazy!

"Ugh...oh, God...please!" I yearned. His lips moved lower, and when they reached my hips, his tongue darted out, tasting me. Little sparks of pleasure began to shoot through my body. Oliver was building my climax, and when I fell, it was going to make my legs buckle beneath me.

"What is it, Beautiful?" he cooed, his tongue licking across the outside of my thigh.

"I can hardly stand," I pleaded, groaning as he pushed his

fingers inside me on purpose. "Oh, please, Oliver!"

Chuckling, he pulled me onto the bed so I was straddling him while he sat upright. "Maybe it's better that you're off your feet for this. Lean back and put your legs over my shoulders. *Holy shit!* I knew what he was going to do next. With his hands supporting my back, I lifted my legs up and over his shoulders. His hands gripped my ass, lifting me so my sex was right in front of his face. Oliver and his obsession with giving me oral—I was a lucky bitch!

"I'm going to take my time, Jade. I'm cherishing you, remember? I don't care how much you beg." I could sense his teasing tone.

His tongue made a long lick across my clit. Throwing my head back, I closed my eyes and became lost to his tongue exploring every inch inside me.

Hours could have passed and I wouldn't have noticed; I was too involved in my feelings. Having to look upside down while Oliver was tasting me was making me dizzy, but I didn't care. My arms were above my head so I could grip the floor for support. That's all I needed. I was building, and any moment now I was going to explode.

"That's it, Beautiful. It's time to give it up—I want it all," he groaned into my sex, running his hands down my chest and over my bra-covered breasts. At his words, I was gone, falling into an abyss of pleasure.

Oliver didn't give me any time to get over my climax. Before I could even blink, he had unwrapped my legs from around his neck and lifted me so my back was finally on his mattress.

"I love this bed," I mused lazily, watching him quickly

strip. "I always have."

"I love *having* you in this bed." I didn't miss the hidden meaning in his words.

"There you go again, bringing everything back to sex."

"Are you complaining?" he smirked, dropping his slacks and boxers at the same time. His cock sprang free, and I licked my lips. *Oh, I definitely wasn't complaining.*

"No," I giggled, watching him crawl up the bed toward me. He grabbed my legs playfully, pulling them apart.

"I'm glad to hear it." He looked down at my chest. "This won't do. You're not naked yet." The moment my bra was removed, his lips latched to my nipples, sucking and biting them both in turn. I began rocking my hips, needing the friction. "Do you want something, Beautiful?" he cooed into my chest, gripping my left breast and sucking my nipple into his mouth. I was done being tease, I wanted him to fuck me!

"Yes, I want that glorious cock of yours inside me, so stop teasing and fuck me." I smiled innocently when he gazed up at me with his mouth slightly open. Yeah, shy Jade didn't speak like that very often.

"There will be no fucking tonight," he grinned, sitting up on his knees. He pulled my aching center toward him, rubbing the tip of his cock in between my folds. "I told you it's all slow and long tonight. I want to feel *everything*." I didn't really care how he was going to take me, all I needed was him and his cock. When I answered with a groan and arched my back, he gripped my hips and gently pushed inside me. "Fuck, how am I going to keep my hands off you while you're working for me, when I know you feel this good?" He had a point.

Oliver's pace was slow and loving, his lips roaming my

body along with his hands. I'd never felt so loved before by a man. When I began to orgasm, he was ready too and we both fell, catching each other in a deep, passionate kiss.

"I'll let you catch your breath first, then I'll fuck you from behind if you still want it fast," he panted in my ear moments later. *Oh, how I loved this man!*

�֍ ✻ ✻

Oliver's bed might possibly have been the most comfortable place I'd ever slept. I lay awake with the morning sun beaming through his huge bay windows, listening to the shower in his bathroom. This place was ridiculously huge for just him.

Having woken up when I felt him leave, I sat up and stretched, deciding to get us both a cup of coffee. It had been quite a late night once we got lost in each other again. I was thankful it was the weekend, but Oliver was still taking me to his office later so I could get comfortable with his computer system and work calendar before Monday.

I could hear Mrs. Davis humming in the kitchen as I descended the staircase in one of Oliver's shirts. I'd need to think about an overnight bag next time I stayed. He was more organized than me.

"Good morning, Mrs. Davis," I called, nervously entering the kitchen.

"Miss Gibbs! Oh, I was wondering when I'd finally see you again," she smiled warmly. "Can I get you anything?"

"I was just getting a cup of coffee for Oliver and myself."

"Here, let me." This kitchen always smells heavenly.

Whether it was coffee, fresh bread, or even bacon, Mrs. Davis looked after Oliver well. "I'm glad you came back to him, Jade. Oliver hasn't been the same man without you. You left quite an impression on him," she commented, handing me the drinks.

"I'm sorry I left in the first place," I admitted, dropping my head.

"This is all a lot to take in. I think anyone would be frightened by it." Why was she so understanding? "I'm about to head out to go shopping now. I've left some fresh fruit and yogurt in the fridge. There's also some pancake mix in the cupboard if the two of you wanted something more filling. Is there anything I can get you while I'm out?"

"No, I'm fine, thank you." I smiled shyly before taking the cups of coffee upstairs. Oliver was almost dressed when I walked into his bedroom. "I thought you might like a cup of coffee?" I smirked, taking in his bare chest before he covered it with a shirt.

"You're wearing one of my shirts again." His eyes were hooded.

"I need to leave an overnight bag like you, I guess," I giggled, handing him his coffee.

"Um...you already have some things here," he winced, moving over to his walk-in closet. I frowned until he pulled out the luggage I left in Macon.

"You kept it? Why?"

"I couldn't bear to throw it away. If I had, it would have been like losing you for good." Oh my! "I think a part of me always knew you'd come back to me." He pulled me into his embrace. "Mrs. Davis washed and pressed everything."

"You do think of everything." I wrapped my arms around

his neck. "I'll have my shower *alone* then," I teased suggestively. "Why didn't you wake me earlier? We could have scrubbed each other's back."

"You looked too beautiful to wake up, and it means I can make a few work calls while you get ready."

"Work on a Saturday?" I pouted.

"You know my office never sleeps," he chuckled, pecking my lips. "Anyway, wasn't last night and twice this morning enough for you?"

"It's never enough," I smoldered, twisting my fingers into his hair. "You know that."

"What have I created?" he laughed, moving his hands to cup my panty covered butt. Oliver had changed me—that was for sure—but not in the way he was thinking. "Go and have a shower. I'll be in my office…and stop tempting me. My cock needs to rest occasionally," he grinned. I pouted, nodding my head. His dirty mouth was making me wetter. "Go!" he snorted. "We'll have time for more of *that* later." With a sly smirk, I slowly began to undo each of the buttons on my shirt. Happy, for once, that I could seduce a man with just one look, I peeled the shirt off my body and let it fall to the floor. Oliver was taking a shower with me—I wasn't taking no for an answer.

"Are you sure you don't want to join me?" I asked innocently, running my hands down my body. He swallowed hard, his eyes raking over my figure, then zooming in on my nipples when I began to tease them with my fingers. "I have an ache, Oliver. Are you really going to make me satisfy it myself?" Within seconds, he was pulling his shirt over his head and dropping his pants. He stalked over to me, lifting me up and swinging me over his shoulder.

"Let's go and see what we can do about that ache." His voice was husky as he raced into the bathroom, closing the door behind us.

* * *

"It all seems pretty organized," I mused, smirking at Oliver. "Alicia may have been a flirt, but she knew what she was doing in this office."

"You're never going to let me live that down, are you?" he snorted. "I was never interested in her in the slightest."

"I can just picture her dropping something by your desk and having to lean down to give you an eye full of her cleavage," I snapped, turning in his seat to look at him as he leaned against his desk next to me.

"You're good at figuring people out, aren't you?" That means she did! "Although, if you're planning on giving me an eye full of *your* cleavage, I wouldn't be opposed to that."

"I told you, while we are working together, there will be boundaries."

"Like what?"

"Firstly, no sex in this office," I replied sternly, crossing my arms. "To be honest, I think we need to be completely hands off when we're at work." Oliver titled his head, pouting. "Don't give me that look. If you want me to work for you, these are the rules."

"Do you really think I'll be able to be completely hands off? We'll be working closely for almost *ten hours* a day." Damn, he had a point.

"Okay, rules don't apply on our lunch break."

"Including sex in the office?" he mused, leaning in to try and kiss my lips.

"No sex in the office at any time!" I giggled, pushing him back with my leg. Oliver grabbed my ankle before I could put my foot back down.

"What about right now? You're not working for me yet."

"No," I laughed, shaking free. "I don't want to walk into this office and think about when you made me cum on your desk."

"I do," he smoldered, trying to get in between my legs. "You seduced me this morning in the shower. It's only right I seduce you here."

"Oliver," I giggled, trying to fight him off. He was impossible sometimes. "That was different. This is your *office*."

"You're really saying no?" he pouted, running his hands up my legs.

"I thought you were going to go through your client and employee lists with me? I need to know who I'm talking to on Monday." Oliver groaned, backing off.

"Okay, no sex in my office," he sulked. It was kind of adorable.

"Except on your birthday," I compromised, turning back to his computer.

"That's only three months away," he whispered in my ear, his fingertips skimming my neck.

"I probably won't be working here then. Now, are you going to show me these client lists or not?" I ordered, trying to change the subject. He was making me horny. Luckily, he finally let it go so we could both concentrate.

* * *

First days at work—I'd had my fair share of them since joining The Seductors, but none had ever been like this. I had to keep reminding myself that this wasn't my real job. I was on a mission...one that I *had* to complete.

Oliver's staff were all very welcoming, offering to assist me in any way they could. Sylvia, Oliver's receptionist, was a Godsend at helping me settle in.

"How's it all going?" Oliver asked as I walked into his office to find out what he wanted for lunch.

"Good. Have I been screening the right calls through to you? Sylvia has been helping me."

"You're doing great, Jade," he beamed. "I'll email you all the changes to my calendar. It looks like we might be taking a trip to Macon at the end of the month."

"Business or pleasure?" I questioned.

"A bit of both," he winked, and when he licked his lips, I had to hold my legs together. We hadn't touched for almost six hours, and my restraint was starting to fail. I was amazed at how well Oliver had done on my first day, but then I knew he respected me *and* his company. He was always professional when it came to his work.

"I came to ask you if you wanted anything for lunch."

"That depends. What's on the menu?" I knew exactly what he was thinking.

"Food, not me," I scolded. "For a CEO, you're easily distracted, Mr. Kirkham."

"I'm *Mr. Kirkham* now, am I?" he chuckled, shaking his

head. "And for your information—you are the *only* one who has ever distracted me at work."

"Maybe you should find a replacement as soon as possible, then?" I suggested innocently, batting my eyelashes.

"Until I know the results of Alicia's test, there's no point. And besides, I like you distracting me."

"Did you want anything for lunch?"

"It would seem what I want isn't on the menu," he grinned. "Why don't you send Sylvia out, anyway? You don't have to get my lunch."

"I want to."

"Surprise me, then," he challenged. *Oh, I loved a challenge.*

It was nice to get some fresh air. I went for the healthier option for both of us with a grilled chicken salad. It was good brain food, after all.

When I walked back to his office half an hour later, I heard a familiar female voice just as I approached.

"We can't talk here, you know that!" Oliver sounded stressed.

"You do realize what this means, don't you?" I was sure it was Macy. As I entered Oliver's office, I saw that I was right. Both of them looked alarmed to see me.

"I'm sorry—have I interrupted something?" I frowned. "I can go and sit with Sylvia if you want?"

"No, Macy was just leaving!" Oliver glared toward her. She was going to respond, but something in his eyes made her stop and leave without even saying goodbye.

"What was all that about?" I frowned, placing his lunch down on his desk. "I got you a grilled chicken salad."

"Thanks," he sighed, running his hands through his hair. "It's nothing for you to worry about. Macy is putting pressure on me about receiving more funding for her and Dylan." I knew I had to press for more.

"Funding for what?"

"Their research. They are extremely close to a breakthrough," he muttered, picking at his food. I could tell his mind was miles away, and I had one guess as to why—Macy and Dylan *were* behind this powercore, and it seemed they'd almost achieved it.

"A breakthrough is good though, right?" Oliver gazed up at me perched on the side of his desk and smiled sadly.

"Not always, Sweetheart," he exhaled, moving his food away before pulling me onto his lap. "I've been dying to touch you for hours," he breathed, inhaling my skin, trying to calm himself. I braced myself, holding his shoulders.

I had no idea how long Oliver held me in complete silence. My hands ran through his hair rhythmically, but I could feel the tension in his body and only wanted to hold him tighter.

He knew the dangers this powercore was going to cause, and it burned me from the inside to know his problems were only just beginning and that I was going to be the route of them.

Now that I was working for him, it would only be a matter of time before I found out if the powercore existed or not, and the location if it did. I was more or less convinced it was Dr. Reynolds making this powercore, simply by Oliver's body language right now. He had the world in his hands and didn't know which way to turn. Time was ticking faster than I wanted it to, and a part of me worried about our future.

Georgie had gotten inside my head more than I realized.

Could I lie to Oliver for the rest of my life, knowing I was the reason his powercore had fallen into the wrong hands? Miles wasn't even sure our client was trustworthy. If it *was* Imogen Windom, he had reason to be worried.

Did I even want to complete this mission for her? If I wanted to keep Oliver and me alive, I had no choice. I was trapped with nowhere to turn. Either way, I was going to hurt the one person I loved more than my own life.

CHAPTER SIXTEEN

Oliver made everything effortless. I'd been working for him for almost six weeks already. We'd even been inseparable in the evenings, too. I was practically living at his luxury apartment, which didn't bother me in the slightest. My past was catching up with me this month through vivid dreams and memories, and I'd never needed him more. If anyone could chase my nightmares away, it was him.

"So?" I asked, trying to gage his reaction. His office was *finally* complete, and I had no idea what he thought of it. "Oliver," I stressed. "Tell me if you hate it. I can redesign it!"

Slowly, he turned around and smirked at me. "Jade, I love it! It's so light and calming. It's just what I needed." *Thank Christ for that!* I'd gone for relaxing pale blues, remembering how much he loved harbours, and added texture with the paintings he'd purchased when he visited me in St. Petersburg.

"Don't do that to me," I scolded, slapping his arm. "I thought you hated it!"

He chuckled, pulling me into his arms and running his hands down my back. "Jade, *you* designed it. How could I *not* love it?" I forced a blush before he crashed his lips against mine. It might have been against work policy, but right then, I'd never needed his lips so badly. I was overjoyed that I could give him this—a part of me that wouldn't ever leave him.

Working closely with Oliver these last few weeks had confirmed my suspicions about Dr. Reynolds and Macy. Oliver was at breaking point with the whole situation. There had been countless secret telephone conversations, meetings, and code names when I passed messages back and forth between Dr. Reynolds and Oliver. It would only be a matter of weeks until he confided in me, I was sure of it. I could feel the stress and tension when we made love. He was trying to lose himself in me, and often did, but when he came back down to earth, I could see it in his eyes. Everything was on his shoulders, and he had nowhere to turn. I wanted him to turn to me, and not just for the sake of the mission.

"I thought this was against the rules," he purred against my mouth, kissing down my jaw.

"We're celebrating you liking your office—I'll make an exception," I giggled, feeling his hands go straight for my butt. "Mr. Kirkham, are you molesting a member of your staff?"

"No," he purred, pulling at my bottom lip with his teeth. "I'm molesting my girlfriend." Why did I love that word so much? I gripped his hair, deepening the kiss before we were disturbed by a male throat being cleared.

"I need to speak with you *alone*, Oliver," Richard glared as we broke apart. I still wasn't in his good graces, and making out with Oliver in his office wasn't going to help.

"I'll get back to those emails," I muttered, dropping my hand from Oliver's concerned face. I didn't want him to start another argument with his uncle because of me, but I could already see it in his dark eyes.

"You need to let this go, Uncle!" I heard Oliver snarl before I closed his door.

"I don't want to argue. You know that was unprofessional," Richard sighed.

"What is your goddamn issue with Jade and me?"

"I feel as if you confide in her more than me. Oliver, I know you're keeping things from me. I'm being kept out of secret meetings, denied access to secure files, and you still haven't explained what project you are funding for Dr. Reynolds!" I shouldn't have been listening, but I couldn't move. "I thought we made big decisions together."

"That was before you held a secret meeting with Imogen Windom behind my back!" Richard did what? How could he be so stupid?

"I only wanted to see what Imogen was offering. Do you have any idea how much power you'd have if you joined forces with her?"

"You are talking complete madness. Do you have any idea what effect that would have on the world's warfare? Imogen Windom isn't the kind of person you'd give *any* control to. You know this! My father warned you so many times!"

"Your father could have been wrong. He wasn't as perfect as you think. He was only human, Oliver. He wasn't infallible."

"Your insecurities toward my father have nothing to do with me. I'm the owner of this company, you are my advisor. You'd do well to remember that, Uncle! You advise! You don't dictate."

"Well, Oliver, you certainly are your father's son. He was always quick to put me in my place, too," Richard sneered. I could hear Oliver yelling back, but I knew I needed to take a step away. This conversation was private between the two of them. I'd often wondered why Richard only had a small claim to Kirkham Industries. I'd recently learned that he was Oliver's father's half brother. Oliver's grandmother had had an affair, and to be honest, Oliver's grandfather had been more than lenient with her and the illegitimate child. Richard grew up thinking he was a full-blooded Kirkham until he was sixteen. I did wonder when or if Oliver would bring it all up, though.

* * *

"What do you want, Beautiful?" Oliver cooed, licking down my rib cage. My skin was clammy from the relentless love making. He was really trying to lose himself tonight, which meant the argument with Richard earlier must have gotten even worse after I stopped listening. They'd been in his office for hours.

"You—I just want you!" I yearned, arching up to him.

"You have me. You know that, right?" he whispered, moving up my body, his nose skimming my hardened nipple. I nodded, running my fingers through his hair.

"I do."

"I need to ask you something, but I'm worried it might scare you away." I was taken aback at his statement. What did he want to ask? Oh, God! Was he going to ask me how I felt about him? Was I ready for that? Yes, I loved him, but I would also be leaving him for a few years in the near future. We had so much to overcome first.

"Just ask me," I breathed, swallowing hard. *Go with your heart, Jade. Oliver has a right to know how you feel about him.* Deep down, I knew I was ready.

"Who is Mina?" *What the fuck!?* How did he know about

Mina? I could feel the blood drain from my face. He knew! Oliver knew everything! Had Richard discovered who I really was? Was that why they'd been in Oliver's office for so long today? "Jade? Baby, you're trembling," he stressed, caressing my face. "I'm sorry. Forget I asked. Just breathe," he cooed while I tried to control myself. I moved onto my side and then sat up, hugging my knees to my chest while feeling my world begin to fall apart around me.

"H...how do you know that name?" I whispered, fear shooting through me. If I failed this mission, we were both as good as dead.

"You've been saying it in your sleep this week. I'm worried about you," he sighed, stroking my back. I relaxed instantly. It wasn't what I thought. We were safe for the time being. "You said her name when you had your nightmare the other night, too." *Shit!* I'd been having frequent flashbacks. I always did when it was close to the anniversary of her death. This month was never easy for me because the memories crept into my dreams often. I could fight them back sometimes, but Oliver's arms had felt like heaven the other night, keeping me safe, making me feel loved after so long.

"She was my older sister," I mumbled, still hugging my knees tight against my body. I couldn't afford to break—not now, not ever.

"You have a sister?"

"I *had* a sister." I swallowed, quickly getting out of bed to grab my robe and put it on.

"Are you running again?" Oliver winced, still sitting on the bed, looking down at his hands. *Run?* Was that what was worrying him?

"No, I was going to make us both some coffee so we can talk," I sighed with a small smile. Was I being serious? Was I going to tell Oliver about Mina?

"You're really ready for that?" he asked worriedly. "If you're not, it can wait. I just want you, Jade. I'm sorry I brought it up. It's just that I've been worried about you."

"I want to tell you parts. I *need* to do this. I've kept this shit inside me for too long. You wanted to know why I run, well, it's because of Mina," I admitted with a shy smile before making my way down his grand staircase. I was being so honest with him, though I wasn't even sure how much I *could* tell him. Georgie was the only person who knew the whole story, but I wanted to confide in Oliver as much as I could. He had a way of making me feel safe, and I knew that was because I loved him. The truth was I had been thinking about confiding in him for weeks. That's what you did with the person you loved, right?

I didn't hear Oliver join me in his kitchen until he wrapped his arms around me from behind. "I know I shouldn't be freaking out, but I'm so worried you'll run after you've told me about your sister." I turned and was greeted by his troubled, dark eyes.

"I'm not running. I can't anymore," I whispered, running my hands down his bare chest and stopping at his heart. The words were on the tip of my tongue, but I fought them back. Telling Oliver I loved him would have to wait. I didn't want to taint it with what I was about to reveal about my past.

"You know I want to believe you—it's habit, ignore me."

"I don't want it to become a habit. You mean everything to me. Why else do you think I came back?"

"Jade, I have to guard my heart—you've already broken

it once. You're here, yet part of me still feels as if you're untouchable...a dream in so many ways. It's been almost a year and still I know nothing about you, but I keep falling." This wasn't how I envisioned the conversation, but I didn't want to change the direction, either. Not yet.

"You're not the only one falling," I whispered, hanging my head. He could be so distracting. I wasn't confessing my love right now; it wasn't the right time. He wouldn't let me look away from him, though. His fingertips tilted my chin, lifting my eyes back to his.

"You want to talk—let's talk," he sighed, taking my hand and leading me into his grand living room. He was about to take a seat on the couch next to me when he suddenly remembered the coffee I had started.

My heart was racing. Mina wasn't an easy topic for me. I was about to bare part of my soul to him—show him a side of me that he might not like. Oliver was going to see my last layer, and the weak, selfish Jade that was trapped deep inside me.

"You're still shaking. Are you sure you don't want something stronger?" he asked, handing me a mug of coffee. I shook my head, taking a deep breath and trying to calm myself. "Take your time, Beautiful. I'm not going anywhere," he soothed, sitting next to me.

We sat in silence for a few minutes because I wasn't sure where to start. I had to be careful not to give actual true events away. My fake family on my Jade Gibb's records were still the same family names I'd had in real life, and just like every other mission I'd ever undertaken in The Seductors, my sister was deceased. It was like losing her all over again with each mission. I shook the thoughts away. They weren't getting me anywhere.

Oliver was still sitting next to me, waiting patiently. *Just go with it, Jade.*

"M...Mina was killed over ten years ago," I muttered, staring into my coffee mug. I heard Oliver's sharp intake of breath and continued. "She was my older sister and I adored her. I was a reckless teenager, always getting into trouble with my dad and stepmom. Mina understood me. She was the only person I ever listened to. I...I never meant..." I began choking on my words as the sobs erupted deep in my chest.

"Jade, Sweetheart. It's okay. Take your time," Oliver soothed. "The moment you want to stop—stop."

I nodded and swallowed, trying to control my whimpers. "I never should have gone to that stupid fucking party," I seethed, forcing my words out. "Mina told me it was a bad idea, but now...I...I have to live with that mistake for the rest of my life. Oliver, Mina is dead...b...because of me. I killed...h...her." My confession brought me to my knees as I slid off the couch, and within seconds, Oliver pulled me onto his lap as the sobs took over my entire body. I couldn't stop the tears as they fell fat and fast down my face.

"Hush, Baby. I've got you," he cooed, rocking me back and forth.

"M...Mina came to get me from the party," I cried into his chest. "She dragged me out of there by my hair. I was so angry with her, I...we argued in the car. She kept asking me to put my seatbelt on and I...re...refused." The pain of remembering was making my chest ache. It felt as if acid was seeping through it, burning all my veins away. "She had to undo her belt to fasten... m...mine." Oliver was still holding me tightly. I knew he must have already worked out what I was going to say next, but I forged on. "I began to struggle, fighting her off. Neither of us saw the other car coming. Mina...Mi...managed to fasten my seatbelt...sec...seconds before the other car hit us head on." His grip on me became tighter. "She didn't stand a chance. She went straight through the windshield and...and...died on impact." With those words, I was done. My whole body was jerking in spasms. I'd killed my sister—the one person I loved more than anything in this world. My father was right. It *should* have been me, not her! I'd already taken my mother from him when I had been born, and then I took Mina. I *was* evil.

I had no idea how long Oliver held me, and when I tried to fight against him, he refused to let me go. He could read my body so well. He knew I needed him...to feel his arms around me, reassuring me, making me think that everything was going to be okay.

"Whatever you think, Jade, you didn't kill your sister. It was an accident. She was looking out for you. That's what family does," Oliver murmured into my hair. "Did you run away? Is that what all of this is about? Why you didn't you want your photo taken by the press? You ran away, didn't you?"

I lifted my head, stunned that he knew me that well. "I wasn't wanted. I'd already caused enough trouble. Running was the easiest thing I'd ever done—I didn't have to face my feelings or come to terms with what I'd caused. I pushed it to the back of my mind. I've only ever told Georgie, and well...it's almost the anniversary of Mina's death. I...I get flashbacks whenever it gets close."

"You're wanted now, Jade." Oliver's voice was hoarse with emotion. My pain was etched all over his face. "You're not alone. I'm here." His lips were quick to mould against mine in a frenzy of lust. My confession had ignited a hunger deep inside me, too. I needed him to take my pain away with his kisses and touch. He was the only man who could make me forget.

"Jade," he moaned, undoing the tie on my robe. His voice was a plea. He knew I'd just bared my soul to him—that I was his.

Rubbing myself against his erection, I was grateful that he was only in sweatpants. I was already naked now that he'd pulled my robe off my body. He stood quickly, lifting me with him, and yanked his sweats off. I couldn't stop grinding my sex against him. I needed any friction I could get.

Our tongues were clashing, our hands roaming everywhere. I had no idea where shy Jade had gone, but I couldn't rein myself in. I wanted him too much.

I pushed him back against the couch, running my nails down his chest, leaving bright red marks. He was already too lost in me to notice as he pulled me over his length. I rocked against him, teasing him, feeling myself become wetter.

"I need you to fuck the shit out of me," I purred against his mouth. "I want you to make me forget everything, even my own name." Oliver thrust up and pulled me down onto his member at the same time as an answer. "Yes!" I cried out, arching back, letting him take control.

His attack was relentless as he pounded into me over and over again. He held my hips tightly, using them to move me up and down his cock. The feeling of him stretching me—claiming me in such a primal way—consumed me. All I could feel was his love for me.

He may have been fucking me senseless, but he took his time, building my orgasm only to deny me the fall. It was driving me crazy. I needed my release.

"Oliver!" I pleaded, digging my nails into his shoulders.

"Not yet, Beautiful. Wait for me. I'm almost there," he groaned, licking and sucking my right nipple. *Wait?* I wasn't sure I could. I was ready to explode.

Just when I thought he couldn't get any deeper, he tilted me back at an angle and I swear I was going to see stars. Hitting *that* spot over and over, I couldn't hold on a moment longer. My orgasm hit me, ripping through my body like a hurricane. I was on sensory overload. He came seconds later, my orgasm setting off his own. *Holy fuck! That was an orgasm!*

Oliver pulled me to him as we both collapsed on the couch, completely spent.

* * *

"Why are you staring at me like that?" he chuckled an hour later. We were still on the couch, wrapped up together in a blanket.

"I like looking at you," I sighed, resting on his chest and gazing up at him.

Lying here with him, content for the first time in my life, I knew one thing; I didn't want to hide my feelings for him anymore. I wasn't going to use my love to trick him into giving up the powercore for The Seductors, though.

I was doing this for *me*. I may be a heartless bitch who killed her own sister, but Oliver knew that and was still here. Surely that gave us hope for the future.

With his love, I could get through anything—even lying to him for the rest of our lives. He was my saviour—the only man to make me feel good about myself in more than ten years. Even if

Jade Gibbs was a lie, she was who I wanted to be when I left The Seductors.

"I like looking at you, too," he sighed, stroking my face. "We should think about going to bed. It's late."

"I am exhausted." I stretched, planting a few soft kisses on his chest before moving off him.

"Wait," Oliver called before I was about to ascend the staircase. I turned, taking him in. The moonlight was caressing his body, and he looked like a dream standing there in just his sweats. "If tonight is the night for confessions, I have one of my own. One that I haven't been able to share with anyone, and it's been eating away at me for months. I need to tell you, Jade, before it drives me insane." *Oh no! No, Oliver, don't tell me about the powercore, please! Not yet!*

"This sounds serious. Do I need to get us both a lager?" I questioned, moving to pick my robe up and put it on.

"I'll get them," he sighed.

"Is this about your uncle?" I asked when he joined me again on the couch. "I'll try harder with him. I'm sorry about earlier. I was so excited about your reaction to your office, I wasn't thinking."

"This is bigger than my uncle, Jade," he sighed, taking a sip of his beer before placing it down on the table. "What I'm about to tell you is top secret—my uncle doesn't even know."

"Oliver, as long as you don't have a secret wife and six children, nothing will shock me." I tried to lighten the mood. He chuckled, but it didn't reach his eyes.

"My company has developed a new nuclear machine." My confession had broken him down. He was about to tell me everything. I just knew it!

"Isn't that what your company is supposed to do?" I frowned, acting confused. As much as I hated it, I had to play him. I needed this information to keep us both alive. I'd never expected my confession to move Oliver like this, though. It was all so wrong.

"This weapon is unlike anything the world has ever seen. I'm playing God, Jade, and I don't know if I'm doing something right or wrong by funding it. In the wrong hands, it will destroy the whole world."

"You said your weapons keep the peace. Why would this one be any different?"

"Its core is different," he muttered, taking another swig of beer. "You're looking at a weapon three times more powerful than any nuclear weapon ever made." I was stunned. He had just confessed. "Say something. Do you think I'm a monster for allowing it to be created?" he stressed, touching my hand. Oliver a monster? Was he insane?

"Why would you think that?" I gasped.

"Macy completed the testing last week. The core works, but there are a few issues with it and we may have to make some adjustments. It's unstable. I won't let her tell Dylan yet, because I'm not sure if I should just abandon the whole thing or not. The world isn't ready for this kind of weapon, Jade. I'm sure of it. I can't be responsible for a war breaking out. It will *kill* me!" I pulled him close, trying to sooth his panic. My suspicions *had* been right about Macy and Dylan.

"You should have told me about this sooner. You can't wear the weight of the world on your shoulders like that."

"What should I do?"

"I don't know." I smiled sadly, running my hands into his

hair.

"I can't keep Macy quiet forever. Dylan will suspect something. I'm stuck. I need to make a decision soon."

"Is that why you were arguing with her last month?"

"Yes. She was angry that I was keeping information from Dylan. I can't help it, though. I haven't known him as long as I've known Macy. I don't trust easily. I can't in my line of work." Yet he trusted me, and I played him. How could I do that to the man I loved?

"Why are you keeping information from him?"

"I'm worried about this core getting into the wrong hands. I've heard a rumour about a secret agency being hired to steal the blueprints to the machine, too." *Composure, Jade!* I was sure all the blood had just drained from my face. "I know it sounds ridiculous. No one could get *that* close to me, but those are the lengths some people will go to gain my weapons."

"Wow! I thought my job had been stressful." My voice was way too high. "Who would want your machines anyway?"

"There are many people, but Imogen Windom would be my first suspect. She's been trying to work with my uncle. The greedy, underhanded bitch." And probably the client I was working for. "Then there's Russia, Japan, and Israel. Any one of them would want this core."

"I'm glad you told me. I want to be there for you, Oliver. You can count on me. Not that I have any idea what you should do, but I hope I've lightened this huge burden for you, at least. I'll never let you down." I meant my words. If there was a way to trick my client with the powercore, I would. There were still so many unanswered questions. Until I knew where the core was being held, coming up with a plan was hopeless.

But one thing was clear. I wasn't going to let my client get their hands on this core unless I really had to. I'd protect Oliver anyway I could, and that included his powercore.

Sonia had been right. This *was* unlike any mission I'd ever been done. For the first time ever, my steal wasn't my priority— my target was.

"I do feel lighter by telling you," Oliver smirked sadly, taking my hand in his.

"I'm sorry I can't be of more help, but you can talk to me about it anytime you want. Night or day."

"That's all I need, Beautiful. Having someone that I know will listen and not judge."

"I'd never judge you—ever."

"It's been quite an eventful night," he murmured, standing up.

"You can say that again," I sighed, letting him lead me upstairs.

"Are you tired?" he asked, slipping into bed next to me once we were in his bedroom.

"Not really," I giggled into his chest. "It's been a crazy night."

"It could get crazier," he smirked. Something told me he wasn't talking about sex this time. "I want to tell you what you mean to me, but I don't want a repeat of last time. I can't ever lose you again. You mean too much to me now. Even more than before."

If there had ever been a time to admit my feelings for Oliver, it was now, so I let the words fall out of my mouth as I drowned in my love for him.

"We need to do it a little differently this time then," I

mused, moving to straddle him. Oliver looked surprised at my sudden action. "I've been fighting my feelings ever since I met you. I'm not running again."

"You've confessed enough tonight. I can wait, I promise. I don't want to put pressure on you. That's where I went wrong the last time. I won't lose you again, Jade."

"No, I want to do this. Oliver, before I met you, I had nothing. No one wanted me or cared, and I was scared you'd wake up one day and not want me, either. But I'm not afraid anymore."

"You'll never need to be afraid. There will *never* come a time that I don't want you. I've never been a selfish man, but with you, I can't help it. You're the one I want for myself. Do you understand what I'm trying to say? I don't care if my uncle or the *whole world* thinks I'm crazy because you're not a nuclear physicist or some high flying, rich business woman. I never wanted that in my partner anyway. You are all I've ever wanted. I knew that the moment I met you."

"I've never felt a love this crippling before. It scares me. I'd do anything for you, to make you happy."

"Jade," he gasped, sitting up.

"I'm madly in love with you, Oliver Kirkham. You know that, right?"

"Yes," he beamed triumphantly, stroking my face softly. "I've known it for a while now." Why wasn't he saying it back? I tried to fight back the panic, but what if he didn't love me after what I'd done to him? No, he'd already admitted it to his uncle; I'd heard him. I was being silly. "What's wrong, Sweetheart?" he asked, tilting my chin up so I had to look at him.

"Y...you haven't said it back."

He moved so we were nose to nose. His hand was in my hair, his sweet breath tickling my face. "Jade, I *never* stopped loving you. Of course, I love you, too." My lips were hard against his, my hands gripping, pulling at his hair. Oliver still loved me. Even though I heard him tell his uncle, I was elated at hearing it directly from him.

We were lost in each other after our declarations, consumed by our love.

I took comfort in his words. With what lay ahead of us, I needed to know he'd be there to catch me, because little did he know, our journey had only just begun.

I had to believe that we'd get the chance to be together, because if we didn't, I would die trying.

Discovering the existence of the power core was still only the beginning of this mission, though. I needed to find its location and gain access to it, but more importantly, I had to find a way to outsmart my client and possibly hand over the wrong core if Oliver decided to abandon the whole thing.

There was still so much to consider, but I knew it wouldn't take long to gain all the answers. Oliver loved me. I was his confidant now. I may have tricked him to get to this point, but I wasn't going to let him down. I would never let him down again.

He was all I hungered for and I'd follow him until the end. Our love, no matter the obstacles, would keep me strong.

ABOUT THE AUTHOR

B. L. Wilde

B.L.Wilde is a UK author. She writes steamy romance. Let your imagination run 'Wilde' with one of her books today.
www.blwilde.com

BOOKS BY THIS AUTHOR

Steel Roses Series

Natasha White has always been unlucky in love. The men she falls for only want one thing from her, and it isn't commitment. When her boss and on/off fling announces his engagement to another woman, she finds herself running from her feelings for him by taking a job as a personal assistant to the legendary rock god, Alex Harbour—half a world away. Her new boss is sexy, damaged, and insatiable, but Natasha has been a fan since she was a young girl. Conflicted by her emotions, she begins a love/hate relationship with the egotistical rock star.

The Human Mating Site

oin Bella, a ray of pure sunshine and an avid steamy romance reader, while she searches for Mr. Right.

Mr. Wimp is the beginning of her story, as she splits from her husband. After twelve years together, Bella never thought she'd be back in the dating pool. She quickly realises how much of herself was lost in her relationship with her ex.

The human mating site isn't so bad, if all you want is some fun to gain your confidence back. Hell, Bella can even act out some of the scenes in the spicy romance books she has read! Online dating is full of amusing plot twists and sexy fun.

Bella soon learns that becoming single in your thirties has never been so sexually liberating.